Miracle

Across the Sound

By Christine Egbert

Betrothed

Messianic Imprint of Little Roni Publishers
Clanton, Alabama
www.littleronipublishers.com

Miracle Across the Sound ISBN 978-1-7359337-5-7
Also available in eBook
v.09072023SC

Cover Designer: ISRAEL KEEFE

PUBLISHED IN THE UNITED STATES OF AMERICA

Dedication

To the righteous men and women of Denmark who honored YHWH, the Giver of Life, by risking their lives to save their Jewish countrymen during the dark days of October in 1943.

PROLOGUE

Berlin, Germany
August, 1943

$\mathcal{D}$r. Werner Best, the former administrative chief of the Gestapo, knocked on Foreign Minister Joachim von Ribbentrop's door, determined to make him understand that this was not the time to enact the Nuremberg laws. Danes were Jew lovers, fanatics about civil rights, and had been for centuries. In 1690 Denmark's Parliament fired the police chief for merely suggesting that they move the Jews into a ghetto. Then they passed a resolution that condemned ghettos as inhuman.

Best sighed at the enormity of the task before him. He must convince Ribbentrop that Berlin's plan to enact these laws at this time would escalate resistance. If that alone failed to sway Ribbentrop, he could remind him that an increase in strikes would gum up Denmark's production. Perhaps he should mention that part first. Best knocked again, harder.

"Come in!" came the reply.

Best entered and gave the salute. "Heil Hitler."

Without rising, Ribbentrop returned it. "The Führer is getting impatient, my friend. He wants your Jews rounded up!"

"I know, I know, but as I explained to you on the phone, these matters cannot be rushed. Denmark is producing well over our quota, and not just in produce, but in parts vital to the Luftwaffe. Why should we rush things and ruin an almost perfect occupation?"

1

The vein on Ribbentrop's left temple bulged. "Perfect? With over 7,000 Jews walking about free! That is not a perfect occupation, my friend!"

"Of course, you are right. You are absolutely right, and it will happen, I promise you. Only now is not the best time, Joachim! You don't know these Danes like I do. They see the Jews as their countrymen, as their friends."

"Do you expect me to tell that to the Führer?" Ribbentrop asked.

Feeling perspiration form on his brow, Best reached for his handkerchief. Their meeting wasn't going as he'd hoped. "No, of course not. Just understand that this will hurt our war effort. These Danes take great pride in their history of religious freedom."

"Stop with all your history lessons! The Führer wants progress! Progress toward his final solution."

"Very well," Best yielded, knowing when he was beat. He replaced his damp handkerchief. "I will start with arrests of any union leaders we can label uncooperative. That should keep Parliament quiet...for now at least."

"This had better work, my friend. Or next time you will hear from the Führer himself." Ribbentrop gave the salute.

Best rose and returned it with as much dignity as he could muster. He clicked his heels, pivoted, and exited Ribbentrop's office, remembering what happened to his predecessor, who was fired the previous November for being "too diplomatic" regarding Jews. Would he be next? That remained to be seen, but one thing was certain. Once arrests began, Goebbels would no longer be touting Denmark as Germany's model protectorate in the international press, nor would that old windbag, Churchill, be able to claim the Danes were Hitler's pampered canary.

The thought brought a smile to his lips, but as Best struck a match to light his cigarette, his smile disappeared. He stared at the flame, searing his conscience for what awaited him in Copenhagen.

Chapter One

At the sound of an engine rumbling on the street, twenty-year-old Fleming Lund froze. He glanced at his watch. It was almost midnight.

"Quick!" he told Inger. "Turn out the lamp."

As he parted the basement curtains, two S.S. officers jumped out of a German staff car. They mounted the steps across the street. Flem held his breath as the taller of the two rapped at the door with his blackjack. A minute later, Mr. Wassermann opened it, still in his pajamas and a robe.

Flem couldn't hear what was said, but even in the dim light he saw the fear on his neighbor's face. The taller of the two officers shoved him aside and barged in.

"Is it them?" Inger asked.

Flem nodded. When Inger began to weep, he pulled her into his arms. He was about to say something comforting when voices out on the street drew him back to the window in time to watch the Germans shove the Wassermann family into the back of the staff car.

Flem felt nauseous. "They're taking them away," he told Inger as he shut the curtain. In the morning, he would ride out to the dock and talk to Katlev. The old man was the only one these days with answers that comforted him…most of the time anyway.

3

"Are they taking them in for questioning?"

"Germans don't question, Inger. They interrogate."

"Lieb's mother says we've been treated with kid gloves, that we should be grateful."

"And just how long do you think it will last?" Flem turned on the lamp. "Until Hitler tires of the pretense and not one second longer."

"It doesn't help to be a pessimist."

"I'm a realist," Flem told her, then he noticed her tears. "For you, I'll put on my rose-tinted glasses." He tilted her chin. "But only if you promise to keep helping me with my flyer."

"You know I will," she said and hugged him.

"We better get busy then. I have a test tomorrow."

Inger wrapped the stencil around the cylinder, then hooked it at one end. Flem fit paper in the tray, recalling his very first edition. In it he'd exposed the fraud the Third Reich had perpetrated on Denmark in 1939 through their worthless non-aggression pact with King Christian. Then, in the wee hours of April 9th, the very next year, German soldiers docked at Langelinie Pier as their paratroopers rained from the sky. Before the sun had risen, Hitler's troops were marching into Jutland.

To their credit, the Danish Army engaged Hitler's troops in a brief skirmish. Even the Royal Guard tried valiantly to defend Amalienborg Palace, but to no avail. Thirteen died and twenty-three were wounded, and the Danish Navy, to their shame, did absolutely nothing. Thus, Germany became Denmark's "protector." Some protection that turned out to be, Flem thought disgustedly. But he knew King Christian had no choice but to submit. The alternative—total destruction—would have been unthinkable.

With a sigh, Flem rotated the cylinder. As it forced the roller to press ink through a stencil, he felt a sense of pride, pride for their courageous merchant seamen, the subject of tonight's edition. At the beginning of the occupation, unlike Denmark's do-nothing Navy, they disobeyed orders, sailing to neutral ports where they joined the Allied Forces.

It had been six months since Flem had turned out that first issue. Since then, he'd reported mostly about the carnage taking place all over Europe, facts he had learned by listening to the B.B.C., an activity strictly verboten by Denmark's German "protectors."

Most of all, he loved reporting on acts of sabotage, which until recently had been far too few. But over the summer, things had heated up. Still, he longed for the day when he would be able to fight Goebbels with more than his father's old mimeograph, which had been collecting dust in the basement until he commandeered it. Now, three nights a week, after his parents were asleep, he and his cousin made flyers.

In the morning, before breakfast, Flem would deposit five packets of forty flyers in their designated hiding places so that members of his group could distribute them.

He had just started proofreading his first page, when the basement door opened. His heart stopped.

"What's going on down there?" his mother demanded.

"Mother! What are you doing up?"

"What am I doing up? You should be the one answering that." Glancing from the flyer to the mimeograph, she let out a gasp then flew down the stairs, with her robe flapping behind her. "What are you doing?"

"We have to get the truth out, Mother."

"About what?"

"About what's happening to our people."

"*Our people* have lived here since 1622. We're Viking Jews!" She pointed to the mimeograph. "And this is how you repay our king?"

"It's not the king I'm repaying."

"What you're doing is illegal, Flem!" She ripped the page out of his hand. "We have a policy of negotiation."

"Negotiation? The Reich pipes a tune, and we dance to it."

"Your father is gainfully employed. He's headmaster of the high school, Flem. We live in this fine house and eat all we want."

"It's only a matter of time before we're relegated to sub-human status like Jews everywhere else."

"I'm going to wake up your father. He needs to see what his son is doing." His mother set her mouth in a hard line then spun around and started back up the stairs.

"Why won't you admit the truth?" Flem asked.

"Cause trouble for them, and we'll get it back double," she said, without turning around. "Do you want to see us dragged out of bed in the middle of the night?"

"The Wassermann family was," Inger said, "just a few minutes ago."

Flem flashed the girl a silencing look.

"Dear God," his mother exclaimed, turning around. She clutched her throat.

"We have to resist," Flem said. "It's our only hope."

"No! Mr. Wassermann must've done something to antagonize them."

"Like what, Mother? Breathing?"

"This is no time for sarcasm, Flem!"

"It's the truth, Mother! Why can't you see it? We have to resist!"

"I heard the Germans are going to enact new laws," Inger said.

"Rumors! Rumors! Always more rumors!" his mother cried. "Let's not give them cause."

"Mother, how can you be so naïve?"

Mrs. Lund rushed back down the stairs and grabbed Flem's arm. "Do you want to see your father forced out of his job? We could lose our citizenship, Flem, our home."

"It'll happen soon enough, Mother, no matter what we do."

"You don't know that, Flem!"

"No, Mother! You don't know it! I do!" he said, yanking free of her grip. "So does everyone else!"

Fury flashed in his mother's eyes. "We'll be sent to a camp if you don't stop this foolishness," she said as a shadow fell across the floor.

Flem glanced up. His father stood at the top of the stairs.

"What's going on down there? A man can't sleep in his own bed," he said descending the stairs.

"Mother's scared," Flem explained.

"The Wassermann family was just arrested," Inger added.

"Is that true, Flem?"

"I'm afraid so, Father."

His mother snatched one of his leaflets and began waving it. "Look at what they're doing, Sol! They're going to get us arrested."

"Calm yourself, Nettie. We won't be arrested if we're careful."

"Don't you understand? These children, these ungrateful children, are printing illegal flyers, Sol."

"They're doing what they have to," his father said, flashing Flem an affirming look.

His mother staggered backwards, as if struck by her husband's words, and bumped against the basket of apples Flem had collected for her strudel.

"You've known about this all along, haven't you, Sol?"

"Have you, Father?" Flem asked, elated.

"I suspected, only suspected," he said with a smile.

Pride swelled in Flem's chest. He should've known it all along. His father was a *mensch*, a real *mensch*!

"You must put a stop to this, Sol!"

"I will not, and neither will you!" He grabbed her hand.

Nettie yanked it away. "You're crazy! All of you! Completely insane!"

"Keep your voice down, Nettie. You'll wake the neighborhood," he warned as a knock sounded at their back door.

Everyone froze.

"It's so late," Inger said. "Who could it be?"

"There's only one way to find out," his father said, maneuvering past his wife. "But I'm certain of one thing. It's not the Gestapo, not at our back door."

Chapter Two

Liesel Prestur shivered as much from fear as the chilly night air. Somewhere in their neighborhood a dog would not stop barking, adding to her angst.

Flem's father opened the door. "Liesel! What on earth are you doing here at this hour? And dressed like that."

She tugged her robe tightly over her nightgown. "Forgive me, Mr. Lund. I was afraid my brother might hear you. There wasn't time to change."

"Well don't just stand there. Come in before you catch cold," he said and stepped aside.

With a rush of emotion, she entered the Lunds' kitchen where until eighteen months ago she had passed so much of her life. Even now, at midnight, it smelled of baking bread. They were all there—Flem, his parents, and the cousin Liesel had heard about.

"Liesel! What are you doing here?" Flem asked.

Liesel knew she must look a sight. She hadn't even stopped to brush her hair.

"Are you all right?" he asked, looking concerned.

"You were all making so much noise," she explained as Flem's teenage cousin shot her a hateful look. What was the girl's problem? "The Wassermann family was just arrested, and I was afraid."

"Afraid of what?" the teenager asked. "You're not Jewish!"

"I was afraid my brother might hear. He's joined the Nazi party."

"Your brother has joined the Nazis?" Mr. Lund asked, incredulous.

"It's his girlfriend's influence. She and her father have warped his mind. Anyway, I had to warn you."

"That was very thoughtful," Flem said, gracing her with a smile. "We also saw the arrest."

"I couldn't sleep after that, so I went down to the kitchen to warm some milk, and Floxy—my cat," she added for Inger's benefit, "started scratching at the door. When I opened it to let him in, I heard your mother shouting about illegal flyers."

Mrs. Lund's face turned alabaster as she slumped into a chair at the kitchen table.

"Aldur is a Nazi?" Mr. Lund repeated. "He was such a good boy, one of my brightest students."

"He's changed a lot, Mr. Lund. I'm ashamed to call him my brother."

Flem squeezed Liesel's shoulder, flooding her with joy. She wanted to throw herself into his arms, only, how could she? Nothing between them had changed.

"Do you think Aldur heard us?" Flem asked.

"He sleeps with his window cracked, so it's possible."

Flem's mother began to weep.

"Get a hold of yourself, Nettie! We don't know if Aldur heard anything. Besides, he's been a Dane longer than he's been a Nazi."

"I wish you would've confided in me about the flyer," Liesel said.

"How could I? We weren't talking," Flem said, looking sad.

"Admit to nothing, Flem!" his mother warned.

Flem made a face. "She's not going to report us, Mother. You'll keep my secret, won't you, Liesel?"

"You know I will...that is, on one condition."

"What's that?" Flem asked.

"Let me help you."

When Flem stared at her, speechless, she wondered what she had said to upset him.

He reached for her hands. "This is a miracle!"

9

Before she could ask him to explain, his cousin placed her hands on her hips. "I'm helping with the mimeograph, so what will she do?"

"We can figure that out tomorrow," Flem told her.

"Don't just stand there, Sol!" Mrs. Lund said. "Do something!"

"If my son finds it necessary to put out a flyer, and this young lady wants to help, I'm not standing in their way."

At that, Flem's cousin stormed out of the kitchen.

Still holding her hand, Flem said, "I'd better see you home. It's getting late."

"It'll be safer if I go alone."

"Are you sure?" he asked, looking disappointed.

"We'll talk tomorrow."

"Come for supper. It's okay. Isn't it, Mother?"

Mrs. Lund rose from her chair. "Ask your father. He's the one making all the decisions around here. I'm going to bed."

"Forgive her, Liesel. I'm afraid my wife has had too much excitement for one night."

"I understand," Liesel said.

"And do come to dinner. I'll cook the meal myself if I have to."

"I will," Liesel promised as Flem let go of her hand to open the door. "Good night," she said, leaving the Lunds' kitchen.

Outside, she paused to lean against the old oak tree where a few years earlier Flem had carved their initials. In the dark, she let her fingers search the bark for the exact place. Something miraculous had just taken place in the Lunds' kitchen. Liesel wasn't quite sure what the miracle was yet, but it didn't matter. All that mattered was that she and Flem were finally talking again.

Joy propelled her across the lawn to the gate that separated their properties. But as soon as she entered her back door and saw her brother standing there glaring at her, her elation turned to dread.

"Where have you been?" he demanded as their cat providentially rubbed up against her leg.

"There you are," she said, bending to pick Floxy up. "Next time you better come when I call you!"

"I asked you a question. Where have you been?"

Liesel ignored him and kept petting the cat.

"Answer me!"

"I was looking for Floxy," she lied.

"What kind of fool do you take me for, Liesel?"

"Now, Aldur, you don't really want me to answer that? Do you?"

"Where were you?"

"I thought Floxy had gotten out. Now, if you will excuse me, I'm going to bed."

"I want an explanation…one that makes sense."

"Or what? You'll have me interrogated by that Nazi gang of yours down at Dagmarhus? I've got a better idea. Why not have me shot?"

~*~*~

The next morning, hoping to be on her way to the university before Aldur woke up, Liesel rose earlier than usual. It had been hard to fall asleep, but once she had, her dreams had been sweet. How could something so wonderful come from something as terrible as the Wassermanns' arrest? Only the Lord could have worked out such a miracle. Flem had called it that too. It was a miracle.

She dressed quickly, paying special attention to her chignon, hoping Flem would like it. She grabbed her satchel. In the hall, she checked her reflection in the mirror. Satisfied, she hurried to the stairs as she reviewed her plan. She would wait for Flem outside the library and invite him to share lunch. It would be just like old times.

~*~*~

The aroma of fresh coffee greeted Liesel as she entered the cheery yellow kitchen. Her father's starched lab coat hung on the back of his chair, and his Bible lay open on the table next to his empty plate. Reading God's Word was as much a part of her father's breakfast this past year as were his eggs. He called it his refueling. Before that, Liesel could hardly remember him ever opening his Bible except at church.

"Good morning, *yndling*."

11

"It's a grand, glorious morning, Father," she said, and planted a kiss on the bald spot on his head. "And I won't be home for supper tonight."

"And why not?" he asked, shutting his Bible.

"I've been invited to eat with the Lunds."

"Our neighbors?"

"What other Lunds would I be speaking of, Father?" Smiling, she opened the cupboard, took down a plate, and laid it on the counter.

"Did Mrs. Lund's niece invite you? She's a bit younger than you, isn't she?"

"Yes, she is younger, and no, she didn't invite me. In fact, I think she dislikes me. Although, I can't figure out why. We've never spoken before last night."

"So why are you eating with the Lunds?"

"Flem invited me."

"Fleming Lund? Oh, *yndling*," her father said, sitting up straighter, "I hope you aren't setting yourself up again."

"I'm sure I don't know what you mean," Liesel said, bristling.

"I don't want to see you get hurt again."

"I thought you liked Flem."

"I do! He's a remarkable young man, but it doesn't change the fact that he is Jewish. You're a Lutheran. And his mother, if I know her at all, will want to find him a nice Jewish girl when he's ready to take a wife."

"Honestly, Father! How positively Nineteenth Century! Marriages aren't arranged anymore."

Her father grabbed her hand. "You know what the Bible says about being unequally yoked."

"We're only sharing a meal."

"A meal today, a life tomorrow."

Liesel threw up her hands. "How can I lead him to the Lord if I don't spend time with him? Besides, if it wasn't for you, I wouldn't have called off our engagement."

Her father's wounded expression made Liesel regret her

12

outburst.

"You need to do some serious praying, *yndling*."

"I have been, Father! I know the Lord's been working on him."

"And how do you know?"

"I just do," Liesel said.

"Oh, *yndling*, I fear for you."

"Well, you should be afraid, but not of my seeing Flem. The S.S. arrested the Wassermann family last night. You should've seen them, Father. It was terrible! I couldn't sleep afterwards."

The furrows on her father's brow deepened. "I was afraid something like this might happen with all these strikes going on."

"All these strikes?"

"Mr. Wassermann is a union boss."

"You're not suggesting Mr. Wassermann brought this on himself?"

"Of course not. It's just that, well, with the strikes going on and sabotage escalating, I'm just not surprised, that's all."

"You're making it sound like our neighbors are responsible, like the Germans are here to keep the peace."

"Nonsense!"

"Next you'll be assuring me the Germans are here to protect us from Winston Churchill."

"I wasn't suggesting anything of the sort, Liesel. Nevertheless, for every action there is a reaction."

"The Germans invaded us, Father!" She swiped at her tears. "They plunder our farms and our factories to feed their war machine. Well, I'm not going to join this pretense that our Parliament is in control."

"Resistance is what's forcing an end to that pretense," he said, pulling out his handkerchief.

"I should hope so!"

"I want you to know how proud I am to have raised a daughter so passionate for justice and so eloquent." He got up and gently wiped away her tears.

"What about your son?"

13

"Your brother can wax eloquent, too. It's his politics," he said with a slight shake of his head, "that worries me."

"It infuriates me!"

"How well I know that." Her father put his handkerchief back in his pocket and sat down again. "Now, if you are quite finished with your diatribe, please explain why you were at the Lunds last night."

Liesel pulled out the chair next to him and sat down. She explained the events that sent her to the Lunds, then began the tricky part. "You see, Father, Flem is responsible for that flyer everyone has been getting. Only his mother didn't know, not until last night, after Mr. Wassermann's arrest. She was angry, and quite loud. So, I had to warn them about Aldur."

Deep furrows etched her father's brow again.

"You won't say anything, will you, Father?"

"No, of course, I won't."

"Once I was there, I realized how silly I've been. Not for calling off the engagement, but for my not speaking to him."

"You had to protect yourself. To give yourself some distance."

"He looked so pleased to see me, Father. He called it a miracle. Actually, it was when I asked to help with the flyer."

"The flyer? No, Liesel! It's far too dangerous."

She took both of his hands. "Weren't you just telling me how proud you are of me?"

As her father's lips slowly formed a smile, Liesel knew he would relent. "Be careful!" he said. "Please be careful!"

"I will, Father," she promised then kissed his bald spot again. When he rose from the table and placed his plate in the sink, Liesel said, "There's more." Her father turned to face her, wearing a worried look again. "Aldur was in the kitchen when I came back. He demanded to know where I'd been. Not only was it after midnight, but I was still in my night clothes."

"Liesel!"

"It's okay, Father. I made up a story about looking for Floxy."

"Did he believe you?"

14

"No."

"Well, I'm not surprised."

"Oh, Father, he hates everyone these days, everyone except Mother."

"I'm not surprised about that either," her father said as if to himself.

"It's that girlfriend of his! She's terrible for him."

"Ursula is a brainwashed child," her father said, refilling his coffee.

"She has certainly brainwashed Aldur."

Her father sighed. "I wish it were that simple, *yndling.*"

"What do you mean?"

"Never mind." He glanced at the clock. "I need to get going, or I'll be late for my rounds."

"Can we continue this later?"

"Absolutely!" he promised.

"Good! Because that son of yours is becoming a real problem."

"I know, *yndling.* How well I know."

Chapter Three

Rounds that morning had been a blur. Juhl Prestur hated not giving his patients the attention they deserved, but how could he? He couldn't concentrate. All he could think about was the conversation he had with his daughter. The Wassermann family got arrested, and Fleming Lund was printing illegal flyers.

Juhl removed his stethoscope and slipped it into his pocket. And, as if that weren't bad enough, his daughter—his only daughter—had reopened a door best left shut.

Juhl sighed deeply. Fleming Lund was a splendid chap but a splendid *Jewish* chap. Mixed marriages of the religious kind were hard enough in normal times, and these times were anything but normal.

Juhl checked his watch to see if there was enough time before his first appointment to pray. There was, and as providence would have it, the chapel was just down the corridor.

Craving guidance from the Lord, Juhl quickened his pace. He had just reached the chapel door when a hand clasped his shoulder.

"We have to talk in private," the man behind him whispered.

Juhl turned around. Dr. Eric Jensen, head of Psychiatry, had deep crevasses etched across his brow.

"What's going on?" Juhl asked.

Jensen glanced both ways, making sure he wasn't overheard. The usually busy hallway had emptied except for one lone orderly passing through the double doors at the far end of the corridor.

16

"Sven Lillelund has been shot."

Juhl's heart skipped a beat. The Lillelund boy was like a son to him. He was always hanging around. Or he had been until he and Aldur parted ways over politics. "How bad is he?" Juhl asked, as they entered the chapel.

"Pretty serious. He and some others blew up a munitions plant. It was this morning's lead story in the paper."

Juhl shut his eyes, trying to make sense of it. "Where's the bullet lodged?"

"In his back, two centimeters from his right lung. He's lost a lot of blood, Juhl. He needs a transfusion. I set him up in O.R. Four."

"But Four is closed."

"Where else could I hide him? We must operate soon. He hasn't much time."

"I don't know, Eric," Juhl said, rubbing his face. "Saving the life of a saboteur? I have a family to think about."

"I can't do this by myself, Juhl."

"What about Dr. Kaufmann?"

"His wife's having a baby."

Juhl began to pace. Aiding saboteurs was a capital offense. His gaze wandered to the plaster of Christ hanging on the cross above the chapel's altar. As a Christian, Juhl knew he was to abide by the law of the land, and Denmark's king had entered into a policy of negotiation with the Germans. Only, not that long ago, he as a Christian had also entered into an agreement—a covenant with God Himself—and God's laws were higher.

Juhl stopped pacing. "I'll have my nurse reschedule my morning appointments."

~*~*~

"Please, can't I stay home today, Aunt Nettie?" Inger pulled the covers up to her chin. "My throat hurts."

Her aunt studied her, brows knitted in concern.

Stricken by conscience, Inger's cheeks burned. She hated lies and hated liars! And she'd just told a whopper. She should have said she

17

felt miserable. That was the truth. She was miserable and had been ever since last night when Liesel barged in. Then, her nightmare in which Flem married the intruder only made her more miserable.

Aunt Nettie sat next to her and placed the back of her hand against Inger's forehead. "You do feel a bit warm."

"I do?" Inger said, surprised. "I mean, yes! I do! I really do feel warm, Aunt Nettie."

"Your face is as red as an apple, child."

Inger, feeling the warmth of her blush, shoved back her covers. "I'm burning up!"

"That's strange. A fever usually starts with chills."

"Oh, I have them too!" Inger stammered, quickly pulling up her covers again.

"Very well. I'll have your uncle explain why you're not in school today." Aunt Nettie rose from the bed. "I'll check in on you again as soon as I get back from the market. If I don't leave now the fish will be picked over."

Inger let out her breath. "Take your time, Aunt Nettie. I'm sure I'll be fine."

"I'll have Dr. Prestur peek in on you when he comes home."

Inger sat up in bed. "There's no need for that." Her aunt stared at her suspiciously. "I mean, well, I'm sure it won't be necessary."

"Inger, I think you better tell me what's really going on. And don't think for a moment that I didn't see the looks you were shooting Liesel last night."

"She's going to spoil everything!"

"Surely, you don't think she'll turn Flem in."

"No, of course I don't!"

"Then what is it?"

"Flem's in love with her! And after last night I know she is too…in love with Flem, I mean."

"That ended a long time ago."

"No, it hasn't, Aunt Nettie." Inger watched as her aunt's face turned ashen. "Well, you saw the way they kept ogling each other, didn't you?"

18

"Well, yes, but—"

"Flem called it a miracle, her being there. He's been praying that she would start talking to him again."

"It can't be! Don't you know why they broke up?"

"Of course, I know! Flem tells me everything!" Inger jumped out of bed and marched over to the window. "It's high time you know what's really going on," Inger declared, pointing to the Presturs' house. Then stricken by her conscience, she dropped her hand.

"Well?" Aunt Nettie urged. "What's really been going on?"

"Never mind. I can't tell you. I promised Flem."

~*~*~

Flem slowed his pedaling as he approached the dock, delighted and surprised to find Katlev's boat there. He'd been so certain that his friend would have put out to sea by now, but he hadn't, and that confirmed that the voice he'd heard earlier, the voice telling him to go now to see Katlev had been HaShem's. Not long ago Flem would have dismissed the episode as nothing more than wishful thinking, but thanks to Katlev's teaching, Flem now recognized the voice of God.

He jumped off his bicycle, filling his lungs with the fresh salt-air. He found his friend in the engine room, up to his beard in grease.

"What are you doing here? Why aren't you at the university?" Katlev asked.

"It's happened! It's finally happened!"

"What?"

"It's something wonderful."

"Well, by all means then, I'll go clean up."

"No," Flem said, "finish what you're doing. I can wait."

"I've done all I can for now." The old man wiped his brow, leaving a fresh streak of grease across his forehead. "The rest will require a real mechanic. The piston is cracked, the edges burned, and there's a hole all the way into the crankcase."

"Sounds serious," Flem said as a wave tossed the boat leeward.

"Nothing the Lord can't handle. Go make us some coffee, and I'll join you as soon as I clean up."

Five minutes later, with the coffeepot just beginning to perc, Flem crossed the cabin to the battered desk on which Katlev kept his Bible. It contained not only the Tenakh, which Flem's Lutheran friends referred to as the Old Testament, but also the Brit Chadasha, the New Testament, which Flem used to think was all lies, until Katlev challenged him to read it, and the Ruach did the rest. Now he knew that the Brit Chadasha wasn't only filled with truth, it was Jewish as well.

When Flem picked up Katlev's Bible, he knocked over a small tin, the kind used to store stationery. The lid came off and yellowed newspaper clippings fluttered onto the deck.

Flem stooped to pick up the tin and its contents, then noticed that a stack of old letters tied with a blue ribbon were still wedged inside the box. The top letter had a German postmark, dated six months ago, and no return address. As he picked up the clippings, he noticed the heading on one of them. It read, "Woman Trampled to Death," and it was dated nearly fifty years ago.

Hearing the old man's footsteps on the stairs, Flem replaced the clippings, set the tin back on the desk, then grabbed the Bible. The coffee was about to boil over. Flem rushed to the stove and turned off the burner.

"So, out with it! What's your wonderful news?"

"Yeshua answered my prayers! Not only is Liesel speaking to me again, she wants to help with the flyer."

"That's a miracle, indeed!" Katlev said, grabbing some mugs out of a cabinet. He set them on the table as Flem brought over the coffeepot. "And so are you a miracle. You're growing in leaps and bounds."

Flem returned Katlev's smile. "It's not that I thought HaShem couldn't do it. I just didn't think that He would."

"His ways are beyond understanding."

"But there's more!" Flem said. "The Lord told me that I'd find you here."

"And where else would I be?"

"Out to sea, by this time of day. Only you weren't."

"HaShem told you about my piston?"

"Not exactly. You see, I was praying, telling the Lord how I couldn't wait to tell you about Liesel, thinking that would be tonight, and I heard Him say, 'Go tell him! Go now!' " Flem reached across the table and placed his hand on his friend's arm. "I would've disregarded God's voice if you hadn't taught me how to listen."

"That's wonderful! I'm so happy for you. And for Liesel. She must be beside herself with joy that you know the voice of the Lord."

"She will be, I'm sure."

"You haven't told her?"

"How could I? My parents were there. But I did tell her she was my miracle. I wish you could have seen her, Katlev. There she was, right in my very own kitchen, in her nightgown and bathrobe."

The old fisherman began chuckling. "That's rather a strange way to pay a visit. But you did ask the Lord to make it memorable, and He certainly did. Now give me all the details. How did this miracle happen?"

For the next ten minutes, Flem related the events of the previous evening. He started with the arrest of the family across the street and ended with Liesel's warning about her brother.

"So, you see, there was no way I could've told her about you convincing me that Yeshua is the Messiah. But she's coming to dinner tonight. I'm sure I'll get a chance when I walk her home."

"What about your parents? When are you going to tell them?"

"Have a heart, Katlev. Liesel and I have just started talking again. Can't I enjoy it for a while?"

"Just don't wait too long, Flem. You know they will be crushed. They won't see this as an epiphany but a betrayal."

At hearing Katlev's words, Flem's elation ebbed. Telling his folks would be one of the hardest things he had ever done. But Elohim, he knew, would make a way. Of that, Flem was certain.

Katlev reached for the newspaper folded on the table. "It appears the Resistance has blown up another factory."

"Isn't it wonderful?" Flem said. "We're finally giving the Germans grief."

"My spirit gets heavier every time I think about this war."

"Why do they hate us, Katlev?"

Katlev let out a sigh. "There are as many reasons as there are people, my boy. But the real answer is that we Jews hold a special place in Elohim's plan. Yeshua came through Judah, and Satan's never forgotten that. But our battle is not against flesh and blood, Flem. When the Enemy comes in like a flood, Ha Shem always raises up a standard against him."

"Then why are so many of us being murdered?" Flem asked.

"A remnant will be saved. There will always be a remnant."

Remembering the verse he'd read the night before, Flem opened Katlev's Bible and flipped to Ephesians. "Here it is, 'the Gentiles should be fellow heirs and of the same body...'" Flem shut the book. "If Gentiles become fellow heirs with us, why do they force us to stop being Jews? The Messiah is Jewish, is He not?"

Katlev smiled.

"Not only that," Flem went on, "but Ephesians 2:12 says Gentiles become part of the commonwealth of Israel. So why do they act like it's the other way around?"

The old man chuckled. "How much time will you give me to answer that one?"

Flem glanced at his wristwatch. "None, I'm afraid. I have to take a test in an hour."

"We'll table it then for next time." Katlev rose and hugged him. "And bring Liesel. I can't wait to meet this miracle of yours."

"I will," he promised.

Pedaling away from the dock, Flem recalled the tin he had knocked over and the newspaper clipping about the woman. Next time, he would try to remember to ask Katlev about it.

~*~*~

Despite his efforts to stem the growing tide of disenchantment with the occupation, Werner Best had failed. Failed miserably!

Summoning the Schalburg Corps back from the Russian front had been a disaster. The Danes saw them not as heroes but as traitors. Sabotage, formerly confined to shipyards, was breaking out everywhere. Dominoes were toppling. There was no turning back.

Since Best had hand-delivered Berlin's ultimatum to Denmark's king, public gatherings were prohibited. A 6 p.m. curfew was enacted, and censorship of the press was now imposed. Firearms and explosives were to be surrendered before September 1st, or those found in possession of them, along with all saboteurs, would be executed.

Harassment of Danes who cooperated with the Reich would no longer be tolerated. Special tribunals had been set up and punishments would be enacted.

Shoving his handkerchief back into his pocket, Best walked over to stare out the window. The phone in his outer office began to ring. Thirty seconds later, a rap sounded at his door.

"Come in," he said.

"King Christian is ready to see you now," his secretary informed him.

"Well, it's about time. Tell him I'll be right there."

"Forgive my presumption, but I already have."

Within minutes, Best stood before the king. He was an impressive figure of a man with a lean aristocratic face and a well-coifed mustache. He'd been parting his hair closer to the middle since the occupation. Perhaps the king was trying to distinguish himself from the Führer. Or perhaps he simply wished to disguise his widow's peak.

Looking grim, the king handed him a document. "Neither my cabinet nor I can agree to these terms."

"You must!" Best replied. "You have no choice!"

"But we do," said the prime minister. "We can resign. And we have. We've dissolved our Parliament."

The vein on Best's right temple began to throb.

"What you do from now on," the king said, "you will do without any support from our government. And I warn you, if you make the

23

mistake of forcing Jewish Danes to wear a yellow star, so will every Dane. I will be the first."

Best's cheeks flamed. "Effective at midnight, martial law will be enforced. Heil Hitler."

When neither the king nor the prime minister returned his salute, Best clicked his heels, pivoted, then stormed out. He knew that his days as Denmark's plenipotentiary were over. At midnight tonight, General von Hannecken would take charge. Then Best would see how much these ungrateful Danes would enjoy their new life.

~*~*~

The second Flem exited his biology class he spotted Liesel waving to him. She looked radiant, like a final burst of summer. The yellow cardigan she wore over her brown pleated skirt highlighted gold strands in her hair. Flem had never seen her more beautiful. He strapped his textbooks together, flung them over his shoulder, and began elbowing his way through the crowd in the hall.

"I need to talk to you," she said breathlessly as he approached her.

"And I have to talk to you," he said, continuing to drink her in. He grabbed her hand. "It's too nice a day to talk here. Let's go outside."

"There's so much I need to tell you."

"Let me go first. You'll be pleased. No, thrilled!" he said, wanting to take her in his arms and kiss her. But that would have to wait.

The sky above them was blue, except for one tiny cloud, as he led her to a bench under an old elm tree. He waited for her to sit. "Remember what you said to me the day we broke up two years ago."

"It was twenty months, to be exact," Liesel said.

Flem smiled. "Nineteen months, three weeks, and four days. I kept count."

"Oh, Flem, I've missed you so much." She grabbed his hand. "We've wasted so much time, haven't we?"

"It wasn't wasted," Flem said. "I'm sure of that now."

"But I was so hateful, so stubborn."

24

"No, Liesel, you were right."

"How can you say that?" she asked, as a lark flapped its wings just above them and soared into the autumn sky.

"Seven months ago, I started working for an old fisherman named Katlev. He's a Jew who believes that Yeshua is the Messiah."

"Well, I assure you, he is not! Jesus is the Messiah! We've been through this all before, Flem." Her eyes brimmed with tears as she turned her face away.

"Please listen to me," Flem begged. "This is important. You'll be pleased, I know you will, once you understand what I am trying to tell you."

Slowly she turned back to face him.

"Yeshua is a Hebrew name. It's a contraction of Yehoshua. You know, Joshua. It means Yah is salvation. Yah is the short form of God's name, which is spelled with the Hebrew letters Yod, Hay, Vav, and Hey. Your Old Testament translates it as LORD in all capitals."

"You mean the tetragrammaton?"

"Exactly! Yeshua means 'Yah is salvation.' He's the one you call Jesus."

Liesel gasped as her face lit up.

Elated, Flem took hold of Liesel's hands. "To make a long story short, thanks to Katlev, I know Yeshua is our Messiah. Katlev proved it to me from two passages in the Prophets—Isaiah 48:16 and Jeremiah 23:5-6. After that, I started reading the book myself."

"The book? What book?"

"The Brit Chadasha, what you call the New Testament."

"You've read the New Testament?"

"All of it, several times."

"And you believe what you've read?"

"I do!"

"And now you're a Christian!"

"Not exactly," Flem said, searching for the right words. "I believe Yeshua is our Jewish Messiah, that he died for our sins, and that the Father resurrected Him. I believe He will return at the end of days, and when He does the dead will be resurrected."

"And those who remain?" Liesel added questioningly.

"Those who remain, who belong to the Messiah, will also be changed. Corruption will put on incorruption."

"Yes! Then we will go to heaven," Liesel exclaimed, "and forever be there with the Lord."

"Scripture says that when the Messiah returns, He and His saints will fight for Jerusalem. The scattered House of Israel will be regathered and joined to the House of Judah, restoring the Kingdom to Israel. Then, Yeshua will reign on His throne in Jerusalem, and Satan will be locked up for 1000 years."

"Isn't that allegorical?"

"Let's not get into that right now. I just want you to know that, as you would say, I've been saved by grace through faith in Messiah."

"Oh, Flem, I'm so happy!" Liesel grabbed him in a hug. "This is a miracle! It's the answer to all my prayers!"

"And you're the answer to mine. I've been wanting to tell you for two weeks now."

"About your conversion? Why didn't you?"

"Well, for one thing, I don't see it as a conversion, not the way you mean it, but just hear me out, okay?

"Okay," she agreed.

"I wanted to be sure, so, I asked Yeshua for a sign, one that would be memorable. And last night, you showed up on my doorstep. Then, when you said, or rather threatened to expose me if I didn't let you help with the flyer, I knew for sure."

"I was only kidding, Flem. You know that, don't you? I wanted a reason to keep seeing you. I've been praying about us, too, you know."

"I'm glad to hear it," Flem replied. "But you almost gave my mother a heart attack."

"I'm sorry. I'll apologize to her tonight, and to your father. Although, he seemed to understand. Your cousin, however, is a whole other matter. I think she hates me."

"Inger doesn't hate you," Flem assured her. "But her attitude disturbed me too. I'm sure she'll come around. I'll talk to her."

"I still don't understand why you waited seven months to tell me all of this."

"I didn't want any distractions."

Liesel's smile faded. "I'm a distraction…"

"Try to understand, Liesel. I had to focus. I had my job to do, school, my flyer, Yeshua."

"Are you sure you have time to fit me in?" she said.

"Don't be that way, Liesel." He stroked her cheek. "It's the right time. You showed up last night, didn't you? You're my fleece before the Lord—you know, like Gideon's fleece."

Her smile returned. "And now nothing can stand in our way."

"Well, I still have to tell my parents about us, and about Yeshua."

"Then we can be married."

"If you'll still have me."

"Have you?" she said. "'Your people will be my people!'"

Flem drew her into his arms and kissed her. After they parted, they were silent for a while.

Then Liesel said, "I'm worried about my brother. My father is at his wits-end. He would've ordered him out of the house last week if Mother hadn't intervened."

"I'm sorry. I know how close the two of you are."

"Not anymore." Liesel lowered her gaze. "He hates everyone except my mother, his girlfriend, and his new Nazi friends. Sometimes I wish father would throw him out."

Flem lifted her chin. "Not because of me, I hope."

"Why must life be so complicated?" she asked, throwing her arms around his neck.

Flem held her. "We're living in crazy times, Liesel. And I'm afraid the worst hasn't begun. All over Europe, Jews have had their lives stripped away. The fact that here in Denmark we still have our citizenship is a miracle. But it won't last much longer. Last month, six Danes were jailed for painting "victory" in French on a German signpost. Acts of sabotage have already tripled from last year and it's only September. We have to take each day as it comes. We have each other, we have our families, and we have Yeshua."

27

"Yes, and I have Aldur!"

Flem lifted her chin. "In this world, you will have tribulation. But be of good cheer, Liesel, Yeshua has overcome the world."

The sparkle returned to her blue eyes. Flem kissed her again. When they parted, he noticed a group of boys heading their way. They sat down on a bench to their left. One of them Flem recognized as the Nazi sympathizer he had had words with the week before.

He grabbed Liesel's hand. "Come on, let's get out of here."

Chapter Four

Flem's stomach was in knots. He tossed his napkin on the table, unable to swallow another bite.

"What's wrong?" his mother asked.

"I've lost my appetite," he told her.

"Lost your appetite? Since when don't you love my Gefilte fish?" she asked, as if she didn't know.

Flem was about to tell her in detail just how disgusted he was with all of her catty comments, when Inger said, "Perhaps Flem would prefer ham."

In all the months the girl had lived with them, Flem had never seen this side of her. He got up from the table. "Let's get out of here, Liesel, before I say something I won't regret."

"Sol! Do something!" his mother pleaded.

"I should do something?" His father looked furious. "You two ladies—and I assure you, I am using the term loosely—have done quite enough. Our son is not the only one who's lost his appetite." Sol Lund threw his napkin on his plate.

"What's happening to us?" Flem's mother cried, pretending bewilderment. But Flem saw through her act.

Staring daggers at his cousin, Flem was about to tell the girl off when she darted out of the dining room in tears.

Liesel stood up. He could see she was fighting back tears as well.

29

"Forgive my wife and niece," his father said. "I don't know what's gotten into them tonight."

"I do," Flem declared, "the Devil!"

At that, his mother indignantly squared her shoulders, rose from the table and walked out of the room.

"I shouldn't have come tonight," Liesel said. "It was a mistake."

"Nonsense. Why shouldn't you eat at our table if my son invites you? I'll get to the bottom of this, I promise you that."

"Thank you, Father. Come on, Liesel, let's get out of here."

The moon shown extra bright as Flem took Liesel's hand and led her to the gazebo. "I've never seen them act this way before, Liesel."

"They must know about our plans and your conversion."

There was that word again, but this wasn't the right time to explain why he hated the word, so he let it go. "Inger knows about us, that's for sure."

"She's obviously told your mother. They're on a mission to derail us."

"We have to get a marriage license right away," Flem said. "Who knows how long, or should I say how soon, it will be before it's illegal for me to marry you. The Reich's enforced its Nuremberg Laws everywhere else they have occupied. I'll speak to my father tonight, right after I take you home."

Liesel shivered. "I wonder what my parents will say when I tell them…and my brother."

"I'll have to drop out of school."

"No, Flem! Don't do that!"

"It'll be okay. I can always go back when this war is finally over. Germany can't occupy us forever, and I think Katlev will take me on full time."

"If you're dropping out then so am I. My father can probably find me work at the hospital. I'm an excellent typist, you know."

"We can discuss that tomorrow," Flem said, squeezing her hand. "I better get you home now so I can speak to my father before he goes to bed and before I lose my nerve."

~*~*~

Flem savored their goodnight kiss at Liesel's back door, then turned for home, determined to tell his father everything. He would lay it all out on the table, from his feelings for Liesel to his faith in Yeshua, even his decision to drop out of school. He'd rather be a fisherman than finish at the university if it meant he could come home to Liesel every night.

His mother would be apoplectic, but that was her problem. As far as he was concerned, she could accept his faith in Yeshua and welcome Liesel into the family as his wife or never see either of them again.

He found his father in his usual chair in the parlor, but unlike other nights, his feet were not up on the hassock. Instead, he sat rigid in his chair. The novel Flem had expected to find in front of his nose lay page-down on his lap.

"We need to talk," Flem said, shutting the double doors. He didn't want his mother or Inger eavesdropping. "I've something to tell you, and please don't try to talk me out of this."

His father ceased staring at the flames in the fireplace and peered at him over his spectacles.

Flem pulled up a chair and sat down in front of him. "Liesel and I are getting married."

His father said nothing. He didn't even blink.

"We're applying for a license tomorrow, and I'm dropping out of school. I can work with Katlev until something better comes along."

Still nothing but silence, deadening silence that turned Flem's excitement to dread. He leaned forward, pressing sweaty palms against his thighs. "Well, aren't you going to say anything, Father?"

"I didn't know I was allowed to."

"Of course you're allowed. I just want you to know that you won't talk me out of this, especially after the way Mother and Inger behaved tonight."

"I've made them promise to apologize."

"Thank you, Father. You're the best! I'm so proud to call you 'Father.' "

"Are you?"

"Of course, I am!"

Sol removed his glasses and tucked them into the breast pocket of his smoking jacket. "I thought that my being Jewish might be an embarrassment for you."

"Embarrassment? Why would you say such a thing, such a crazy thing?"

His father shrugged. "Inger tells me you've been praying to Jesus."

Flem slapped his forehead. "Inger! I should've known." He would deal with her later.

"Well? What have you to say for yourself?" his father asked.

"I've been praying to Yeshua, the Jewish Messiah."

"Jewish Messiah?"

"Father, I can take you scripture by scripture and prove that he is the Messiah. Or I could have Katlev do it. He's a very learned man."

His father's eyebrows arched. "A learned fisherman? I'm impressed."

"Years ago, he studied to become a rabbi."

"And he became a Lutheran instead," his father said dryly.

Flem let that go. "You would like him, Father. I know you would if you would just give him a chance. He's a remarkable man."

"More than remarkable! He's a magician," his father said. "He turns Jews into Lutherans."

"A Jew who worships the Jewish Messiah doesn't stop being a Jew, Father!"

Sol jumped to his feet. " '*Shema Yisra'el, Adonai eloheinu, Adonai echad.*' A Jew worships *one* God! Not three!"

"I don't worship three gods! *Echad* is a compound unity! Read Isaiah 48:16! 'Come near to Me and hear this. From the beginning, from the time that it was, I was there. And now Adonai Elohim"— Flem shot up one finger—"and His Spirit"—he shot up a second—

"has sent Me." Flem shot up a third. "How much clearer can it be, Father? Read Isaiah for yourself! Isaiah 48:16. Elohim is a plural. God said, 'Let Us make man in Our image.'"

"The Messiah, the Jewish Messiah," his father bellowed, shaking his index finger toward heaven, "will regather Israel! He will bring peace. This Jesus of yours has done neither! If anything, it's gotten worse!"

"But, Father, even the Zohar teaches that there are three powers in heaven, three powers that are *Echad*! A compound unity! For centuries great rabbis have taught there would be two Messiahs, the suffering-servant and the conquering king. Only it won't be two Messiahs, but two visitations. Yeshua already came as the suffering servant. He'll return as Israel's Conquering King! That's when He will regather the tribes and restore the Kingdom."

"Our Messiah, the Jewish Messiah, won't do away with the Torah. Your Jesus did!"

"He didn't! I know that's what Christians think, but I've read the Book, the Brit Chadasha. Yeshua said, that until heaven and earth pass away and all the Torah and the Prophets have been fulfilled not one jot or tittle will pass from the Torah or the prophets."

His father threw his arms in the air. His face was so red that Flem feared he might have a stroke. "Jews who pray to Jesus are no longer Jews! They are Christians! Now excuse me, I'm going to bed."

"Christian is Greek for a follower of the Messiah," Flem said, blocking his father's way. "Jewish believers were the first to be called Christians! Gentiles who come to faith in Israel's Messiah get grafted in and become a part of the commonwealth of Israel. Jews don't stop being Jews. It's Gentiles who stop being Gentiles. At least that's how it's supposed to be according to the Book."

"What commonwealth? There is no commonwealth! There is only Palestine, and it's controlled by the British."

"Well, there was a commonwealth when Paul wrote to the Ephesians. And one day there will be again."

"Britain's king has declared 'unequivocally' that Palestine will never become a Jewish state," his father said. "Jewish immigration and land transfers have been restricted. In another ten years Palestine will have been granted independence."

"But, Father, the Irgun party is calling for massive Jewish immigration. They want to form a Jewish commonwealth."

"Well, I've called for an end to this war! But, my dear deluded son, the Germans are still here, and they're in full control!"

"But they won't be here forever, and right now in Palestine thousands of Jewish volunteers are joining British forces to fight the Nazis."

"Stop clouding the issue! My son, my only son, is no longer a Jew. But what does that matter? If Hitler and the Mufti have their way, there won't be any Jews left anywhere."

"There will always be Jews, Father! And one day there will be an Israel again."

"When it materializes," his father said, "we can talk about it. For now, I've heard enough. I'm going to bed."

Chapter Five

Liesel awoke the next morning to the annoying cuckooing of the clock above her bookcase. She was amazed that she'd been able to sleep at all with so much on her mind. She and Flem were getting married! They were getting the license that very day. Talk about miracles! A few days ago, they weren't speaking, hadn't spoken in nearly two years. She jumped out of bed. It amazed her how quickly life could change.

She glanced at the clock. Flem would be calling for her in half an hour. She would have to hurry to be ready to leave the moment he got there. She didn't want any run-ins with Aldur.

She said her morning prayers while she changed. Not wanting to draw her brother's attention, she resisted the urge to put on her best dress, choosing instead a simple sweater and skirt. She let her hair hang loose about her shoulders.

Twenty-five minutes later, she dashed down the stairs. She entered the kitchen gliding on air, then noticed her family. They all sat at the table. Her mother looked pale. Her father's face was red. Aldur alone looked pleased as they listened to the radio.

"What's going on?" Liesel asked.

"General von Hannecken is addressing us," Aldur replied, waving his hand to silence her.

"Martial law has been declared," her father explained. He pulled out a chair for her to join them.

"The Danish government has demonstrated its inability to maintain order, so now the Wehrmacht will," the general continued. "In accordance with Articles 42-56 of the Hague Convention, respecting the laws and customs of war on land, I declare a military state of emergency in the whole of Denmark, with immediate effect."

"Civil servants shall continue in the performance of all duties. They shall comply with the directions given by the appointed German authorities. Crowds of greater than five persons in public and private are forbidden. Closing hours are at sunset. A curfew will be imposed. Use of the mail, telegraph, or the telephone is temporarily prohibited until further notice. And a ban is imposed on all strikes. Strikes further the interests of the enemy and will be punishable by death."

Liesel's eyes burned with tears. How could this be happening? She was so close to marrying Flem. It wasn't fair! It just was not fair!

"Danish citizens who comply with these laws," the German general droned on, "will continue to enjoy the protection of their person and property."

Liesel covered her ears. She had to get away. She jumped out of her chair, ran up to her room, and locked the door. Then she threw herself across her bed, sobbing uncontrollably.

A few minutes later, someone knocked. "*Yndling*, let me in," her father said. "I want to talk to you."

"I can't. Not now, Father."

"*Yndling*, open the door."

After several seconds, she forced her body off the bed and unlocked the door.

Her father took her in his arms. "It's hard for all of us, Liesel, but God will see us through this."

"But you don't know all that's happened, Father! The timing couldn't be worse."

"For some things there is never a good time."

"But you don't understand. Flem has accepted Christ. He's asked me to marry him. We were supposed to get the license this morning."

"But this is so sudden."

Liesel pulled away from him, went back, and sat on her bed. "We should've been married last May, Father."

Sitting next to her, he draped his arm around her. "But you only started speaking to him the other day."

"I've been in love with him most of my life, and I'm almost twenty. Only the differences in our faith kept us apart, and that's no longer a problem."

"But, *yndling*..."

"I thought you, of all people, would be happy for me, Father," she said, releasing another sob.

"I am happy for you, *yndling*, and for Flem." He handed her his handkerchief. "Or I will be once I digest all these changes."

"Did that general say anything about Jews being forbidden to marry Gentiles?"

"Not that I recall."

"Then Flem and I can still be married," she said as someone gently tapped at her door.

"Flem is downstairs, Liesel. What should I tell him?"

"Tell him I'll be down in a second, Mother." Determined to see their plan through, she dashed over to her vanity to repair her face. The last thing she needed was for her brother to become suspicious.

"May I tell your mother?" her father asked rising from her bed.

"Please do! Only not in front of Aldur. He can't know anything until after the ceremony."

"Who is performing the marriage?"

"I'm not sure. It's the one thing we've not yet discussed. Do you think Pastor Uri would agree?"

"I can ask him."

"Oh, would you, Father? Would you?"

"I'll see him this afternoon, provided I can get away from the hospital. But what about Flem's parents? Do they know?"

"Flem was supposed to tell his father last night."

"Where will you live?"

"I'm not sure, but Flem will be leaving school. So will I."

"No, Liesel! You mustn't."

"We'll get jobs, Father. It will be fine. But I have to go now."
She kissed his cheek and ran out of her bedroom.

At the bottom of the stairs, Flem's face was a mask of restraint,
except for his eyes. They glistened with love.

Aldur lurked in the hallway, watching them.

Liesel tried to feign calm. "Ready to go, Flem?"

"My bicycle is parked out front."

"Good. I'll go get mine."

"Riding together again, are you?" Aldur asked, popping a stick
of chewing gum into his mouth. "I must say, sister dear, it's a rather
strange time you've picked to renew your friendship with this Jew."

Gritting her teeth, Liesel walked up to her brother and slapped
him hard across the face.

When Aldur grabbed her wrist, Flem stepped between them.
"Let her go!" he said.

"How dare you threaten me in my own house, you Kike!"

"Aldur! Let your sister go!" her father ordered, thundering down
the stairs.

Matching his father's stormy look, Aldur released her.

But Liesel wasn't ready to call it quits. "If you ever speak to Flem
like that again—or about him—I promise you, I'll forget I ever had
a brother." High on adrenalin, Liesel latched onto Flem's arm. "Let's
go. The air in this house is polluted."

The two marched out the door, but the second it shut, Liesel
began trembling. What was happening to her family? Aldur and Flem
had never been close, but they had never been enemies. Her
brother's attitude left her mortified. She had wanted to choke him.

Flem took her in his arms.

"I don't know him anymore, Flem. Ursula has corrupted him."

"I know," he whispered. When her tears subsided, he kissed her.
"Let's go get your bicycle."

"Did you tell your father?"

"I did," he said as they left the front porch.

"Well, what did he say?"

"What could he say? I wasn't exactly asking for his permission."

"Then he must be against us, too! I thought he at least liked me."

"He does. It's Yeshua he's upset about," Flem explained as they headed around the house. "Or I should say it's my insisting that I'm still a Jew."

"Oh, Flem, things keep piling up."

"Father will come around. We have to be patient. I'm sure my cousin Inger has cast everything in the worst possible light."

Liesel stopped walking. "What has Inger to do with this?"

Flem stopped and placed his hands on her shoulders. "She got to Father before I did. I made a mistake, confiding in her about you."

"About me?"

"Including why we broke up." Flem lifted her chin. "I had to tell someone, Liesel. I was miserable. Inger was supportive. At least, she was until I told her about Katlev. She thinks he's *meshuga*. That's Yiddish for crazy."

"Just because of his faith?"

"She knew what I was praying for. When you asked to join our group, she must have realized we'd be getting back together."

"So that's why she kept shooting me those looks." It all made sense now. Except for one thing. "Is Inger in love with you?"

"In love with me? No! No, of course not! Don't be ridiculous! What a notion. We're cousins for pity's sake."

Liesel smiled at Flem's naivety. "Inger wouldn't be the first girl who ever fell in love—puppy love—with her cousin, her older, witty, and extremely handsome cousin."

"Oh, stop it," he said.

"She's lost her parents. She's vulnerable, hungry for love, and susceptible to your charms."

Flem squared his shoulders. "You make it sound as if I've seduced her."

"I don't mean to, Flem. Only, try to understand it from her point of view. After all, I was in love with you at her age."

"That's different!" Flem said, looking indignant. "You're different. We're different. She's my cousin, and she's only a girl."

39

"Girls fall in love, or they think they do. Who knows what dreams she might have been nurturing until I showed up on your doorstep?"

Finally, he smiled. "You were the answer to my prayers. Come on, let's get your bike. If we get to City Hall early enough, we should have fewer problems. Although, with this new state of affairs, it's hard to say what could happen."

~*~*~

The historical square, Flem's favorite part of town, was usually busy, but this morning Copenhagen's cobblestone streets were ominously deserted. Tivoli amusement park, where four years earlier Flem had kissed Liesel on top of the old Ferris wheel, still dominated the square in spite of armed German soldiers. Exchanging a fond look with Liesel, Flem remembered their first kiss as the couple pedaled past the park. Dagmarhus, designed to resemble a Renaissance structure, lay just ahead. The historical edifice, which had long housed Copenhagen's City Hall, was now also the headquarters of the Third Reich.

"Maybe we better not go in," Liesel whispered to Flem as they walked their bicycles along the sidewalk to the racks.

"Don't you want to marry me?" Flem teased.

"You know I do."

"Then don't let them intimidate you. We're here. Let's do this."

Inside the building, the corridors were deserted except for a soldier pacing in front of a doorway down the hall. Holding his breath, Flem took Liesel's hand. As they entered the empty licensing office, he noticed the Reich's new regulations were posted in bold print at the main desk.

The clerk stopped filing papers and looked up at them. "Yes. May I help you?"

"We'd like a marriage license," Flem said.

The clerk glanced furtively at the doorway as the sentry passed by. "Then you'll need to fill out an application." Lowering his voice, he added, "Have you heard what's happened?"

"It's the only thing on the radio," Flem whispered back. "It's preempted everything."

The clerk leaned in closer and lowered his voice more. "I mean what happened over at the Navy Yard. Admiral Vedel gave orders for our fleet to scuttle our ships or escape to Sweden."

"That's wonderful!" Liesel said just before the sentry passed by their door again.

"You can fill out the form here or have a seat to do it."

"We'll fill it out here," Flem said.

As the clerk slipped him the form, another soldier approached the sentry, who was now standing in the doorway. The two exchanged a few words in German, then left, heading in opposite directions.

"They've ordered us to continue doing our jobs as usual. Only now we're to report to one of their magistrates. You're the first applicants in here all morning. Everyone's too afraid, I suppose."

"Can Jews still marry Aryans?" Flem asked, keeping his voice low.

The clerk's eyebrows shot up. "Are you Jewish?"

"Flem is," Liesel said.

"You better hurry then. I'll process your license immediately."

When Flem and Liesel exited City Hall twenty minutes later, they passed a group of reporters who were peppering a contingency of scowling German dignitaries with questions. Flem recognized one of them as Germany's Plenipotentiary to Denmark, Werner Best. He looked quite tired, as if he'd been up all night.

~*~*~

Upon entering the conference room, Best ordered the doors locked. As second in command now, under General von Hannecken, he had to make it clear he was not without clout.

"The Danish press has managed to impart the ridiculous idea that Germany is weak. The proclamation issued to the public this morning should put an end to that nonsense. Every editor from now on will be responsible to see that Danes are no longer being poisoned by these seditious ideas."

"Is it true," someone from the press asked, "that the Reich has taken hundreds of high-ranking officials, including military officers, as hostages?"

"We've done only what is necessary to maintain order," Best replied.

"Is our king a prisoner of war?"

"He is under our protection."

"What about our Navy? Rumor has it that over twenty of our ships were scuttled."

Best silenced them with a raised arm. "I am not here to answer your questions. Your country is occupied! It is time you Danes start acting like it. This press conference is over."

Chapter Six

Eager to introduce the woman he loved to the man who changed his life, Flem hopped off his bike, grateful for the broken crankshaft that kept his mentor from putting out to sea. He hoisted their bicycles into the boat, then helped Liesel on board.

"Ahoy," Flem called. "Anyone home?"

"Down here, my friend," came the familiar reply from inside the cabin. "You're just in time to help me mend some of the nets."

Flem grabbed Liesel's hand and led her down some steps. "I have someone with me that I want you to meet."

On the far side of the cabin, Katlev laid down his needle on a table burdened with fishing nets and rose to his feet. His bearded face could not hide his wide grin as he extended his arm. "You must be Liesel Prestur."

"I am," she said, taking his hand.

Flem treasured the moment. "Soon she will be Mrs. Fleming Lund." He waved the license as proof. "God's miracles never cease."

Katlev beamed. "*Mazel tov! Mi Adir al hakol, Mi baruch al hakol, Mi gadol al hakol, Hu y'vareykh et he'khatan v'et ha'kalah.*"

Liesel turned to Flem, half amused, half bewildered. "What did he say?"

"He who is supremely mighty, He who is supremely blessed, He who is supremely sublime, may He bless the Groom and Bride. It's recited at Jewish weddings."

43

"Well, now, this calls for a toast," Katlev said. "Flem, my boy, get down three glasses, and I'll get us some wine to celebrate."

Katlev cleared the table and piled his nets in a corner. A few minutes later, he handed Flem and Liesel each a glass then raised his. "May your union be as blessed as mine was with Sarah."

Liesel looked confused. "Was?"

The twinkle in the old man's eyes dimmed slightly. "She passed on two years ago."

"I'm so sorry," Liesel said.

"There is nothing to be sorry about. Sarah will rise again at the resurrection. Besides, we had a good life and a wonderful marriage. You know, rabbinic tradition teaches that a marriage will be peaceful only if the Most High is in the union."

"We Lutherans believe that, too," Liesel said.

"The Hebrew word for man is *ish*," Katlev continued, "and for woman it's *isha*. The man's name contains the Hebrew letter *yod*, and the woman's the letter *hey*. Together the *yod* and *hey* spell *Yah*. It's the Hebrew contraction for Yahweh."

"The personal, and according to the rabbis unspeakable, name of HaShem," Flem explained.

"True," Katlev said, "but I am no longer so certain that His name should not be spoken, but I will save that for another time. You see, Liesel, when a man and a woman come together in marriage, only Yah can make them one, *echad*. If you remove Yah from their union, you are left with the Hebrew word for fire—*aish*."

"That's wonderful," Liesel said.

Flem squeezed her hand. "I told you he was amazing, didn't I?"

Katlev raised his glass. "To the bride and the groom. May you always be *echad*. *Mazel tov!*"

All three took a sip.

"It seems strange, being so festive," Liesel said as she set her glass down, "considering what's happened today."

"What do you mean?" Katlev asked.

"Haven't you heard?" Flem asked. "Parliament has resigned. Martial law has been declared. Whoever goes on strike from now on will be executed. The whole town is swarming with German soldiers. I thought you knew."

"I'm so sorry for the two of you. At a time like this, you should be planning what to name your first child, not worrying if…"

"If what," Liesel asked.

"If it might be born in a concentration camp," Katlev said.

Liesel knitted her brows. "Surely, they won't try that here!"

"Why wouldn't they?" Flem asked. "For months now, I have been warning that this was coming." He reached for Liesel's hand.

Liesel glanced from Flem to Katlev. "What's wrong with you two? We might not have a government, but we still have our God, and He's mightier than these Nazis!

"Your bride-to-be puts me to shame," Katlev said. "You'll have to stay on your toes with this one, my boy."

Bursting with pride, Flem put his arm around her.

"Now, that's better," she said, looking delighted by Katlev's remark.

"So, tell me about the plans for your wedding," Katlev urged.

"Father's going to ask our pastor to perform the ceremony," Liesel explained.

"How do your parents feel about that, Flem? Will they attend?"

Flem shrugged. "They attended a church wedding three years ago for a cousin of mine. I hope they'll do as much for their only son, once their shock wears off."

"I have an idea," Liesel said. "Why don't we incorporate some of your Jewish traditions into our wedding ceremony? We can have Katlev and pastor Uri co-officiate."

The suggestion intrigued Flem. "It might make my folks feel more comfortable, at that."

"But I'm not a rabbi," Katlev said.

"You almost were," Flem reminded him. "And I would love it!" It was what he'd always wanted, to stand under the *chuppah* with his bride.

"Well, if you both insist. I just hope your pastor agrees with your request."

Liesel jumped out of her seat and hugged the old man. "It'll be beautiful, the best wedding Copenhagen has ever seen."

Flem sighed. "Well, that solves one problem, but I still need a job."

"You have a job," Katlev said.

"I'll need a full-time job. I'm dropping out of school."

"But you only have a year left," Katlev said.

"I'll have a wife to support sooner than that. Besides, I can always go back later, or go to night school."

Katlev's smile faded. "Do you know how many have thought that and never did?"

"I'm quitting, too," Liesel said. "My husband will be my career."

"So? Can you use me or not?" Flem asked.

Katlev gazed at him a second longer, then shrugged. "Why not? You can start as soon as I get my crankshaft repaired."

Flem grabbed his friend in a bear hug. "You won't regret this, Katlev, I promise."

"I'm a fortunate fellow to be blessed with you two in my life, and now one of you will be my partner." He raised his glass in a toast. "To new beginnings."

Flem and Liesel raised theirs.

"I'm grateful to finally have someone in my life who is happy that I'm marrying Flem."

"Your parents aren't happy about your engagement?" Katlev asked.

"Father would be, I think. He's just concerned about the timing, and Mother, well, I'm not sure what she'll say."

"You haven't told her?" Katlev said.

"I was going to this morning, but when I heard the radio…well, let's just say nothing has gone according to plan today. But Father has promised to speak to her. I just hope my brother doesn't find out."

"He's joined the Nazi Party," Flem explained.

Liesel sighed. "Yes, you should've heard him ranting about Flem this morning. He was disgusting."

"Do you think he'll cause problems?" Katlev asked.

Liesel shrugged. "Who knows? All I can do is pray that he doesn't."

Flem checked his watch. "It's getting late. We better go."

"Do we have time to ride by the church?" she asked. "I'd like to speak to Pastor Uri myself."

"I thought your father was doing that," Flem said.

"He is, but he doesn't know about Katlev."

"We better hurry then."

"Call me at home tonight and let me know if the pastor agrees to her proposition."

"I won't be able to. Telephone calls have been restricted until further notice, but I'll ride over to let you know."

"Before sunset," Katlev warned.

~*~*~

Liesel's excitement was an intoxicating mixture of fear and euphoria as she and Flem peddled their bicycles along Copenhagen's newly deserted cobblestone streets. German soldiers patrolled every corner. Liesel had not seen such a large number of soldiers around since the early days of the occupation.

When they reached the church, she spotted her father's automobile parked at the curb. It gave her a sense of security as she and Flem fastened their bikes to the rack on the side of the church.

"Isn't that your father's Citroen?" Flem asked.

"It is, and I'm so glad he's still here. Now I can find out what my mother thinks of our getting married. Only, before we go back to the rectory, I want to show you the church."

Flem let go of her hand and opened one of the massive sandstone double doors.

Liesel could not wait to find out what Flem thought of their sanctuary's architecture which combined gothic with baroque. Ribbed brick arches vaulted two rows of squared pillars that supported the roof. The nave and the semi-circular choir lay beneath its great spire.

The church's half-rounded windows, in spite of their great size, let in little light, especially on cloudy days like this, but it was still adequate to show off the magnificent craftsmanship of all the statuary depicting Jesus and His apostles.

"So? What do you think?" she asked.

Flem didn't answer. He just looked around.

"Don't you like it?"

"It's beautiful, but…"

"But what?"

"There isn't time to get into it now, Liesel." Flem took hold of her hands.

"Get into what? You love art! You love architecture! You love beautiful things!"

"You're the most beautiful thing in here, and I love you."

"I don't understand you at times, Flem. Well, come on. Let's go see Pastor Uri."

Her father met them as they rounded the walkway to the rectory. "What are you two doing here?" he asked, looking surprised.

"We came to speak to Pastor Uri about the wedding," she said.

"I thought I was taking care of that. Hello, Flem."

Flem nodded.

"You are, Father, only something has come up."

He looked concerned. "Not another problem."

"It's not a problem. Just my brilliant idea."

"In that case, we better go back to the rectory. We shouldn't be talking out here."

In silence, they followed the stone path past the church office. When they reached the parsonage, her father tapped at the door. A moment later, Pastor Uri's wife opened it.

"Did you forget something, Doctor?" she asked. Her expression changed as soon as she saw Flem.

"It's okay, Ana," her father replied. "This is Fleming Lund, the young man I was telling you about."

Ana stepped aside and let them in. "You're getting a wonderful girl," she said.

Flem smiled, but Liesel could see she was nervous.

"I know, and thank you," Flem said.

In all the years Liesel had been a member of Pastor Uri's parish, never once had she been inside his home. Its furnishings, though of quality, looked worn and belonged to the previous century.

Pastor Uri rushed in from the kitchen. "Has something happened?"

"Not at all," her father assured him.

The pastor's expression relaxed, but only slightly.

"It's this awful martial law, isn't it?" Liesel said. "You both look so tense. I can't believe it has finally come to this."

Pastor Uri nodded. "It's a terrible state of affairs."

"We need to tell them everything. We can trust them."

"Well, if you're certain," the pastor said, not sounding convinced.

"Tell us what?" Flem asked. "What's going on?"

Mrs. Uri waved them to the sofa. Liesel and Flem took the love seat as her father removed his glasses and vigorously polished them with his handkerchief.

"Father, please. Just tell us what's going on."

"Sven Lillelund has been shot."

"Who is he?" Flem asked.

"He's my brother's best friend, or he was before Aldur became a Nazi. We'll have to go to the hospital and see him."

"He's not there. He's here. I had no choice. He and some others blew up that munitions factory you read about in the paper. Lillelund took a bullet in his back. I removed it yesterday. It was too risky to keep him in the hospital. Pastor Uri graciously has agreed to care for him until I can arrange for a boat to smuggle him into Sweden."

"Why not ask Katlev?" Flem suggested. "I'm sure he'd be willing to do it."

"Oh, Flem," Liesel said, "what a wonderful idea!"

"I might even go with them myself," Flem said.

"No, Flem, it's too dangerous!"

"I am Katlev's partner now."

Liesel sighed. At least he would have to wait for Katlev's crankshaft to get fixed and for Sven to heal. "May I see him, Father?

"Why not? Only, don't stay too long," her father cautioned. "The lad needs his rest, and I have to get back to the hospital. So, if we need to discuss anything else, let's get it over with."

"There is," Liesel said. "I have a brilliant idea for the wedding."

"I've already agreed to do the ceremony," Pastor Uri told her. "Nothing could give me more pleasure. And you are joining the Lutheran Church at the perfect time, if you know what I mean," he told Flem.

"Thank you, Pastor Uri, but my faith in Yeshua isn't—"

"He means Jesus," Liesel explained.

"It isn't for political expediency. I am a Jew, and I will always be a Jew."

Pastor Uri looked confused. "I'm afraid I don't understand."

"What Flem means," Liesel said, "is that he is a Christian-Jew."

"A Christian-Jew? I've never heard of such a thing."

"Of course, you have, Pastor. What was Peter?" Liesel asked.

The pastor's face turned as red as a boiled ham. "Well, yes, but there are no Christian Jews today. It's unheard of."

"Why is that?" Flem asked.

"It just is, that's all. That sort of syncretism would create all kinds of problems. For instance, where will you worship?"

"I have no problem with attending your church if that's what Liesel wants. But I must be perfectly honest. I am and will always be Jewish. A Jew who believes in the Jewish Messiah is still a Jew. And I will still keep the Sabbath and all of God's Feast Days."

Liesel looked at him. They had never broached this subject before. A long silence ensued.

Finally, Pastor Uri shrugged. "Well, if Liesel doesn't mind, who am I to complain? It seems odd to me, that's all."

Looking pleased, Flem reached for Liesel's hand. "We were hoping to incorporate some Jewish traditions, some Hebrew prayers and blessings, into our ceremony."

"You want a Jewish wedding?" Pastor Uri asked.

"Katlev Hertz—the man who led my fiancé to the Lord—studied for a time to become a rabbi. We would both like it very much if he could, well, co-officiate."

"Co-officiate?" Pastor Uri repeated, sounding bewildered.

"You and Father will love him," Liesel assured him. "He's a dear old man, a fisherman as crusty as Peter himself. It would mean so much to both of us."

"It's their wedding, dear," Ana Uri said. "What could it hurt?"

The pastor shrugged. "How soon do you want the ceremony to take place?"

"Right away," Liesel said.

Flem squeezed her hand. "I've been thinking maybe we should wait a few weeks. We have the license. The Reich can't stop us as long as they don't find out. But we need a place to live, and I haven't started working fulltime yet. What kind of husband would I be if I can't provide a roof over your head?"

"You could live with us," her father suggested. "Just until you get on your feet."

"Thanks, Doctor Prestur, but after what happened with Aldur this morning, I don't think that would be a good solution. And my parents' house, I'm afraid, won't be much better. We need a place of our own. I hope you understand."

"Of course," her father said.

"Well, I don't!" Liesel fought back tears. "It will be torture enough waiting four days, let alone four weeks. I thought you wanted to marry me!"

"Of course, I want to marry you."

"Then why wait? A lot can happen in a month," she said, remembering the armed German soldiers patrolling the streets.

"The Lord has kept us for these past two years. He can certainly keep us for four more weeks. Where's your faith?" Flem asked.

"He's right, *yndling*. Be proud that you have a man with such integrity and faith. You must let him have his way in this."

Liesel knew her father was right. She just hoped it wasn't his way of keeping them apart longer.

"The time will pass quickly," he assured her. "And it wouldn't hurt for you to spend a little time in the kitchen with your mother. You might learn a few things. You know that old saying about the way to a man's heart."

Liesel smiled begrudgingly. "Then it's Flem's mother I better start spending time with. Don't you think?"

Everyone laughed. But Liesel knew, after the reception she'd received from Flem's mother the night before, such mentoring would not take place anytime soon. Prayer and even fasting would be required to make Mrs. Lund willingly share her culinary secrets with her soon-to-be daughter-in-law, her soon-to-be Christian daughter-in-law.

Her father glanced at his watch. "I better get back to the hospital. Remember what I said about not tiring Sven. The boy needs his rest, and whatever you do, don't discuss anything that was said here today with Aldur."

Chapter Seven

Late that afternoon, Flem rode over to Katlev's, eager to tell his friend about his visit to Liesel's pastor. The roads in town, although no longer deserted by Danes, were still clogged with German soldiers. Only on Katlev's street was there nary a Nazi to be found.

"Why don't we go into the kitchen?" Katlev suggested. "I was about to have my supper. Care to join me in a little øllebrød?"

"Thanks, but I've already eaten. It smells wonderful, though. I didn't know you could cook."

"When a man becomes a widower, he either learns to cook, or he starves. Fortunately for me, my dear wife collected recipe books."

Flem smiled, trying to imagine Katlev cooking at a stove.

The table was set for one. Katlev pulled out a chair. "Have a seat. And tell me how things went at the church."

"Pastor Uri agreed," Flem said, purposely leaving out the awkward exchange that took place. "We have four weeks before the wedding, so you have plenty of time to work out the details about the ceremony with Liesel."

"Four weeks? I thought you'd be tying the knot sooner."

"I'm going to need a month to earn enough money to rent a place for us to live."

"What about here? With Sarah gone, the old house has more space than I need, and it wouldn't cost you an ore."

53

His suggestion took Flem by surprise, but he loved the idea as he looked around. The stove and refrigerator were smaller than his folk's and the place needed modernizing, but it wasn't without a certain charm.

"Just help out with the groceries and light bill, and we will call it even. What do you say?"

Flem wanted to grab Katlev in a bear hug, but he restrained himself. "Naturally, I will have to discuss it with Liesel, but this might be our answer. Thanks, Katlev! You are an answer to prayer."

"An answer to prayer? Well, what could be better than that? Wonderful! Wonderful!" He turned to the stove and dished up his soup. "Are you sure you won't try some?"

It smelled delicious. "Well, maybe just a bite."

Katlev took down another bowl. He filled it to the brim and set it on the table. Øllebrød, what Danes called beer soup, was one of Flem's favorites.

Katlev opened a drawer and handed him a spoon.

Flem tasted it. "You really made this yourself? It's delicious."

Katlev shrugged, looking quite proud. "The pumpernickel, I soaked it in ale overnight. There wasn't much to do after that but to add some lemon, water, sugar, a little cream, and let it simmer."

"You'll have to teach Liesel," Flem said, refilling his spoon.

"Be glad to."

"There is one other thing." Flem hated having to request another favor. Katlev had already been so generous. "Do you know about that munitions factory the Resistance blew up a few days ago?"

Katlev nodded. "It was in the paper."

Flem lowered his voice. "Dr. Prestur removed a bullet from one of the saboteurs. It was too dangerous to keep him in the hospital, so he took him to Pastor Uri's."

"And you want to bring him here?"

"We want you to smuggle him to Sweden."

"Oh, I see…"

"It's his only chance, Katlev."

The old man laid down his spoon, looking thoughtful.

"If you can't, perhaps you know someone who could?"

When Katlev stared into his soup in silence, Flem chided himself. He should never have put Katlev on the spot like this. The risks were too high, and the man had already done so much. Flem was about to tell Katlev to forget it, when the old man began stroking his beard.

"The Sound is only a few miles across at strategic points," he said. "We'll have to leave at night." Katlev stopped fidgeting with his beard and faced Flem. "We must pray that clouds will cover the moon and keep our eyes peeled for German patrol boats."

"Thank you, Katlev."

Katlev raised his hand. "The most important thing we must do is fast and pray!"

~*~*~

Liesel peered through the window in her bedroom, fingers tingling from clutching the curtain too long. Curfew was to start in fifteen minutes, and Flem had still not returned. She released the curtain. Oh, why had she not insisted he wait until tomorrow to speak to Katlev? If anything happened to him, she would never forgive herself, and neither would Flem's family.

She opened and closed her hand, trying to return circulation to her fingers. Then through the lace, she spotted a bicycle. As it turned onto their street, Liesel's heart slammed into her ribs. It was Flem! He was pedaling so fast his spokes were a blur.

Letting out a shriek, she bolted from her room.

"Is the house on fire?" Aldur called from his bedroom.

Ignoring him, Liesel flew down the stairs, brushed past her mother in the hall, then darted out the front door. Flem was walking his bike around the side of his parents' house.

"What took you so long? I've been worried to death."

"I have ten minutes before the curfew," he said, looking amused.

"So, what did he say?"

"I'll tell you inside. I have something I want to give you first, something in a box."

Anticipation replaced pique. "What is it?" she asked, praying it would be a ring.

"Patience, you'll see."

Flem opened the shed and pulled the cord hanging from the ceiling. The light came on, and he parked his bike next to the lawnmower.

Liesel looked around impressed by the assorted boxes neatly labeled on all the shelves. Flem's mother's reputation for being organized was certainly not an exaggeration, but the only box Liesel cared to see at the moment was the one Flem had mentioned. She was quite certain it was not one of these.

"Can't you give me a hint?"

Gracing her with a wide, mischievous grin, Flem said, "It's from Katlev."

"From Katlev?" she repeated, deflating like a pierced balloon. "Is it something Jewish?"

"I can't tell you out here. I want everything to be perfect."

Hope flickered in her again, only now she was really confused. Flem spoke like a fellow about to give his girl a ring, but why would it come from Katlev?

As twilight faded into night, Flem took her hand and led her along the path. When they reached his back steps, he turned to face her. "So, you were worried about me, were you?"

"You know I was."

"I'm glad. I like hearing it."

Smiling, Liesel snatched his cap off his head as they entered the Lunds' kitchen, where Inger sat at the table with a book opened in front of her.

"What's she doing here?" his cousin asked, shooting Liesel a deadly look.

"She has a name! Kindly use it in the future," Flem said.

Liesel was now certain she'd been right. The girl was in love with Flem. It was the only thing that made any sense.

Inger slammed her textbook shut. "Are we still doing your flyer?"

"Not till things settle down. Where are my parents?"

"Uncle Sol's in the parlor. Your mother is upstairs mending socks. She's been worried sick. Have you forgotten about the curfew?"

"Of course not," he said, tugging Liesel toward the hallway.

"Then don't you think your girlfriend should go home?"

"She's right, Flem. I should go."

"Relax! I'll take you home later. There aren't any patrols on our street."

"But Aldur saw me leave. He'll know I came here."

Flem looked impatient. "He's your brother, for goodness sake!"

"And a Nazi," Liesel reminded him.

"Do you want to see what I have for you or not?"

"Of course, I do," she said, trying to ignore Inger's hateful stare.

"Then let's go!"

Halfway down the hallway, they made a right turn into the Lunds' dining room. Flem felt along the wall for the switch. Finding it, he turned on the light. As she entered the dining room, Liesel wondered which of the sterling silver candlesticks on the sideboard Mrs. Lund used to light her Sabbath candles.

Flem pulled out a chair. He waited for her to sit, then reached into his pocket. Watching her expression, he pulled out a tiny box and knelt as he opened it. "Will you marry me?"

Tears welled in Liesel's eyes.

"It belonged to Katlev's wife. He insisted I take it. You don't mind, do you, Liesel?"

"Mind? Of course not! Well, put it on!" she said excitedly. "Let's see if it fits."

The gold band slipped onto her finger with ease.

"It was made for you, Liesel," Flem said beaming. Then they both heard a gasp.

Flem's mother stood in the doorway looking horrified. "You're already married?" she asked.

"No, Mother! Not yet."

Liesel quickly removed the ring and handed it back to Flem.

"But we will be very soon," Flem told her as he put the ring back in the box. "Didn't Father tell you?"

Ignoring Flem, Mrs. Lund glared at Liesel. "If you think by converting my son you will spare him from Hitler's wrath, you'll be sorely disappointed."

"Liesel had nothing to do with my faith in Yeshua, Mother. Not the way you think anyway. You can thank Katlev for that, and Katlev is a Jew."

"If he were a Jew, a real Jew, he wouldn't be proselytizing," she retorted.

"I love your son, Mrs. Lund. I'll do everything I can to make him a good wife."

As Flem's mother began sobbing, Liesel's own eyes filled with tears.

"For what are you crying?" his mother asked. "You aren't losing your son, your only son."

"We're supposed to rejoice with those who rejoice and weep with those who weep." Liesel put her hand on the woman's shoulder. "Believe me, Mrs. Lund, I never meant to hurt you. I only want to be your daughter-in-law, like Ruth was to Naomi."

Flem handed his mother his handkerchief.

"I'm sorry," she finally said, directing her apology to Liesel. "I don't mean to be so hateful. It's just that, well, please just forgive me."

"Of course, I forgive you," Liesel answered.

"I'm just so scared. Everything is changing so fast. Where will it all end?"

"Put your trust in the Lord," Liesel encouraged her. "He will keep you in perfect peace."

"You mean your Christian god, Jesus?"

Not sure how to answer that without escalating things, Liesel shot Flem a beseeching look.

"She was quoting from Isaiah, Mother. Isaiah is in the Tenakh," Flem explained as his father rushed into the room like a storm cloud about to burst. Inger was right behind him, wearing a satisfied smirk.

"Our son was just showing me their ring, Sol," Mrs. Lund explained in a shaky voice.

"What were you saying about the Christian god?" Flem's father demanded.

"I quoted a verse from the book of Isaiah, and Mrs. Lund thought it was from the New Testament."

"I don't want you proselytizing my wife. Is that understood?"

"Mother was stressed, Father. Liesel was only trying to help."

"Help?" Mr. Lund said. "Is that what you call this?"

"I better go," Liesel said, fighting back tears.

Flem grabbed her arm. "No! Wait!" He turned to face his father. "In a month, Liesel will be my wife. You can either accept her as your daughter-in-law or lose me as your son."

"Of course, we'll accept her," Mrs. Lund said. "Go on, Sol, tell them. Your cousin has a mixed marriage, and they've never had a problem."

"A mixed marriage, I can deal with, but my cousin is still a Jew."

"So am I, Father!"

Flem's father raised his fist in a threatening manner but Mrs. Lund stopped him from landing a blow.

"Let's go, Liesel," Flem said. "I'm taking you home then coming back to pack. I'm moving in with Katlev."

"You can't leave tonight!" Inger said, looking horrified. "There's a curfew!"

"Then first thing tomorrow," Flem declared.

"Do something, Sol," Mrs. Lund begged. "He's our only child."

"He's not my child. My son was a Jew. I have no idea who this imposter is. At least Nazis don't hide their true intentions."

Dear God, Liesel prayed. Help us! Help us all!

Chapter Eight

"Of course, you can move in," Katlev exclaimed. "Haven't I already offered you and your bride-to-be a home here?"

"I knew I could count on you. Thanks, Katlev!" Flem grabbed his bike off the pier and hauled it onto the boat.

"I guess that means Liesel has accepted my offer," the old man said, but as Flem's smile faded, he began assuming the worst. "Did she turn my offer down?"

"She never got the chance. I didn't have time to tell her after the blow up with my folks."

"Oh, I see…then there's still hope."

"It springs eternal," Flem said. "Or so I've been told."

"But deferred, it makes the heart sick. Now tell me why you're moving in this early. What's happened?"

"It's my father. Everything was going okay until he burst in on us. I had just given Liesel the ring when my mother came into the room. She saw the ring and thought we'd already tied the knot and went to pieces. But Liesel calmed her down. You should have seen her, Katlev. Liesel was magnificent. She would've had Mother eating out of her hand if my father hadn't come in when he did."

"That's wonderful, Flem! You're getting a terrific girl. As for your father, well, there is nothing that Elohim can't fix."

"I just don't understand him. The night before, he was the rational one, at dinner at least, before my brat-cousin got to him. Do

60

you know what he said to me? He said I was worse than a Nazi or something to that effect."

"He didn't mean it, Flem. He's just scared."

"That's what my mother said."

"That your father was scared?"

"No, that she was. Our neighbors' arrest has shaken her."

Katlev nodded with understanding. "Come on, let's get some coffee."

Down in the cabin, Flem slunk into his usual spot at the table. Katlev took two mugs out of the cabinet, then reheated the leftover coffee on the stove. Neither man spoke for a long while.

Katlev poured the coffee as Flem stared into space, elbows on the table and his knuckles cradling his chin.

"Was it wrong for Sven to blow up that munitions factory, Katlev? After all, we have a policy of negotiation with the Germans."

"You don't ask easy questions, my boy."

"You can handle it."

Katlev stroked his beard. How could he answer without sounding hypocritical? "The king had no choice. You know that, Flem. You wrote about it often enough in your flyers."

"But doesn't God want us to obey the law?"

"The Nazis want to annihilate us. We have a right, a God-given right, to defend ourselves."

"But Sven's not a Jew."

"Does he have to be Jewish to resist evil? Why do you think he joined the Resistance?"

"But it's wrong to break the law."

"And it's right to resist evil! And evil men make evil laws. Sven didn't start this war, Flem. Hitler did. What did Peter and John do when the Sanhedrin ordered them not to teach in Yeshua's name?"

"They refused to comply."

"Exactly! And Rahab hid two of Israel's spies then lied to save their lives. Does that mean God approves of lying? No! Yet Rahab is called a hero of the faith, is she not?"

"It's so confusing…"

"We have to distinguish good from evil, the Father's voice from the Adversary's, Flem!"

"I know, and I do."

"Good! You had me worried there for a minute."

Flem looked insulted. "Come on, you know that I support the Resistance. I'm putting out an illegal flyer. I just want to make sure that Elohim approves of what we're doing."

Katlev relaxed. He could certainly understand that. "Well, just remember the Lord hates evil and loves justice. Evil men love evil. And they will win if we don't stop them."

Flem smacked the table. "Edmund Burke! 'The one condition necessary for evil to triumph is for good men to do nothing.' I was just studying him the other day."

"Exactly! And that's why we must take a stand."

Flem raised his coffee mug. "Well, if we're caught smuggling Sven into Sweden, the Germans will execute us. I think that qualifies as taking a stand."

Katlev laughed. "It certainly is my boy! It certainly is!"

~*~*~

The kitchen was Liesel's favorite room. It had several windows that filled the house with light on cloudless days. Doing the breakfast dishes was not a chore when the sun's rays warmed her face. It was the perfect time to pray to the Father of Lights, in whom there was no shadow of turning.

She had just dried the last dish and was about to put it in the cupboard, when her brother came into the room.

"Well, look who we have here, and all alone. Where's your boyfriend, little sister?"

"Don't start with me, Aldur!" she said, then turned to leave. But Aldur blocked her way, so she stepped aside.

"Get out of my way!"

"What's the matter, sister dear? Don't you want to talk about your Jew boyfriend?"

"You make me sick!"

"Or is it because you were out after curfew last night?"

"You better remember what father told you!"

"Father's not here now. So, why not tell me what you and your Jew boyfriend have been up to."

Furious, she drew her hand back to slap his face, but Aldur was too fast. He grabbed her wrist. "Don't ever try that again. Not if you know what's good for you."

"Then don't ascribe your morals to me. You're the one with a trollop for a girlfriend."

Aldur's fingernails dug into her wrist. "Take that back!"

"Why should I? You aren't the only one who loves Germans. Your girlfriend does too, especially German soldiers, and everyone knows it."

"Take it back, I said."

"How does Ursula find time for you?" Liesel asked, unable to stop herself, as Aldur's nails dug deeper into her flesh. When he began twisting her arm, Liesel cried out in pain.

"Aldur! Let your sister go!" Her mother stood in the doorway dressed in her bathrobe. Her hair was still wrapped in a towel.

With a shove, Aldur released her, causing Liesel to stumble against the counter. Her arm struck her mother's sugar bowl. It shattered on the floor, scattering the sugar everywhere.

"Now see what you made me do!" Liesel cried.

"What on earth is going on in here?" her mother demanded. "I could hear you two up in the bathroom."

"Your son doesn't like hearing the truth about his trollop of a girlfriend," Liesel said, rubbing her wrist.

Aldur stepped toward her, in a threatening way, and her mother stepped between them.

"My son, as you call him, is your brother. I wish both of you would remember that!"

"He started it!" Liesel said.

"Isn't there enough hate in the world without you two going at each other's throats? Now clean up this mess so I can go back and finish washing my hair."

"Sorry, Mother," Aldur said, acting contrite, but Liesel saw through him. Why couldn't her mother see that he was feigning remorse?

"I need to speak to you before you leave for the university, Liesel."

Liesel bit her tongue, wanting to shout I'm not going to the university, but her mother had already left the room.

Her father, evidently, had not told her mother yet about her plans to marry Flem. For now, she would have to hold her tongue, but she could no longer hold back her tears. Five minutes ago, she was basking in the glow of love. Love for Flem, love for the Lord. Now, she felt defiled by hate, or something close to it. These things, she knew, should not be.

Chapter Nine

George F. Duckwitz stared out his fourth-floor office window. In the early morning mist, everything appeared normal. Boats bobbed rhythmically along the docks as seagulls swooped and dipped into the Sound hoping to catch a herring for breakfast. Everything went on as if nothing had happened, as if nothing had changed. Only, George knew that it had. And more upheaval was on the way. Of that, George was certain, and it troubled him greatly.

For fifteen years, he had lived a good life there in Copenhagen. For fifteen years the Danes had accepted him, made him feel like a native son. Now, George was ashamed, ashamed to be German, ashamed to be a member of the Reich's Embassy staff.

Heart heavy, he returned to his desk, wishing his boss, Werner Best, had not confided in him about the Führer's demand that he solve Denmark's Jewish problem. Jewish problem indeed! Denmark had no Jewish problem! Copenhagen's Jews were assimilated. More than assimilated, they were an integral part, an asset to Denmark. George had friends, wonderful friends, who were Jewish. He had had them since he moved here in 1928.

No, there was no Jewish problem, not here in Denmark! But there would be if Hitler did not stop his insanity. George was certain of it. And Hitler's problem would not be only with Denmark's Jews. Every Dane would rise up. George knew these Danes and their sensibilities.

Why, just this January, George had witnessed their boldness first-hand at a songfest in Gjorslev. A university student had requested the audience's participation in singing two national anthems. The first was Denmark's own—no surprise there. The second one, however, had caused the Reich's dignitaries to nearly fall out of their seats when a student unfurled the Zionist flag. The crowd, still on their feet, belted out *Hatikvah*. The memory made George smile. What did they expect? That Danes would sing *Deutschland Uber Alles*?

No, there was no Jewish problem in Denmark, no need for Der Führer's final solution. George had tried to make that clear to Werner Best, but it had done little good. Now it was time to try something else.

He opened the top drawer of his desk and removed his address book. Having found the listing for the Social Democrat Headquarters, George lifted his phone's receiver to his ear and dialed the number.

"Good morning. Is Hans Hetoft available? He is? Wonderful! Yes, tell him George Duckwitz, with Reich Shipping, would like to speak to him. Yes, it's important, very important!"

~*~*~

Later that morning, after Liesel had prayed through and washed away the defilement she had felt earlier, brought on by her altercation with her brother, she fortified herself with a hot cup of chamomile tea and sat down at the kitchen table across from her mother. The tea, she hoped, would help her to maintain her calm as she listened to whatever it was her mother wanted to talk to her about.

"Your father will be upset when he finds out I've told you. We had hoped to spare you the ugliness,"—her mother took a deep breath—"but with you and your brother at each other's throats all the time now, well, it's better that I tell you everything now. This way you won't find out from your brother in another fit of rage. Besides, you're almost a married woman."

"So, Father told you about our plans?"

"Yes, but I don't want to discuss them now. I need to talk to you about Aldur."

"What has he done this time?"

"Aldur has done nothing. He's a victim in all of this."

"Aldur, a victim? How can you say that, Mother? A monster, yes! Or, at best, a fool, but not a victim!" Her mother's heartbroken stare unnerved her. "I'm sorry," Liesel said. "Go on. I'm listening."

"Remember when I went to visit my sister in the Shetland Islands?"

Liesel nodded. How could she forget? Her father had taken to haunting the house like a ghost, aimlessly wandering the halls in the middle of the night, irritable and preoccupied.

"I wasn't at all certain that I would ever come back."

"Not come back! Mother, what are you saying?"

"There's no delicate way for me to put this, dear, so here goes: your father had an affair."

"Father? I don't believe you!" Her father was a paragon of virtue devoted to his family.

"The young woman was his patient. She was only a few years older than you when she got pregnant. But your father wouldn't divorce me to marry her. So, she committed suicide."

"You're making this up."

"I wish I were, Liesel. Unfortunately, it happened. In all fairness to your father, he tried to end the affair after the first encounter. But then the young woman threatened to go public. It continued for several weeks, and the woman became pregnant."

"Did you know this was going on?"

"No, dear, not at the time."

"I can't believe it," Liesel whispered through her tears.

"He promised to have our lawyer set up a trust fund for the child, but insisted he never wanted to see her again."

"And she killed herself."

"Not then. She made the mistake of going to see the hospital administrator. Mr. Andersen told her he would have her arrested for extortion."

"Extortion?"

"It turns out, she had tried this once before with another married doctor, who paid her a tidy sum to go away and have her child."

"She already had a child?" This was worse than a French novel, Liesel thought, hardly able to take it all in.

"Conveniently, the woman had miscarried, or so she claimed, after cashing the check, of course." Her mother rolled her eyes. "Anyway, Mr. Anderson summoned your father to his office and told him about the visit. He told your father that forty was too old for him to be sowing wild oats, and that if anything like this ever happened again, he would be dismissed. Two weeks later, a letter arrived at your father's office. In it, Gisele—that was the woman's name—threatened to kill herself. She said she hoped it would haunt Juhl the rest of his life, and that he deserved it for using her so badly."

Liesel's head was spinning. It was all so sordid. "But how does this have anything to do with Aldur?"

"I'm getting to that," her mother said. "Aldur came into your father's office, right after he finished reading Gisele's letter. He folded it and laid it on his desk, but when your brother left the letter was gone."

"Gone where?"

Her mother shrugged. "Your father thought it had somehow gotten mixed in with Aldur's books. So, he rushed home and searched your brother's room, but he couldn't find it. It had simply disappeared. Knowing it could still turn up, your father confessed everything to me that night."

"I am so sorry, Mother!" Liesel got up and hugged her. "Can you ever forgive me?"

"Forgive you for what?"

"For not believing you."

"Oh, sweetheart, I understand. I really do."

Finally, Liesel released her. "And the woman really killed herself?"

"She ran her car into a tree the next day. According to the autopsy she was pregnant."

The weight of her mother's words rested heavily on Liesel's heart. "I need some more tea. Can I get you some?"

"No, dear. I'm fine."

"Is that when you went to visit your sister?"

"It is."

"No wonder you weren't sure you would ever come back—it all makes sense now—why Father was so distraught."

"He wrote me every day," she said as Liesel poured scalding water over the tea bag in her cup. "He begged my forgiveness. Nothing like this had ever happened before, he assured me, and it never would again. He begged me to come home, in every letter, but I just couldn't. I felt betrayed."

"But you did come home," Liesel said, sitting down.

"After Juhl confessed to Pastor Uri, he recommitted himself to the Lord and to our marriage."

"So that's why Father reads his Bible all the time now."

"Your father's faith in the Lord changed him, and it softened my heart, made me able to forgive him."

"I'm so glad, Mother. But I still don't see how Aldur figures into all of this."

Her mother's eyes filled with tears. "While I was away, your brother found Gisele's letter. Somehow it had gotten stuck between the jacket and cover of one of his textbooks. He was furious when he found it. He confronted your father."

"So that's why he's been so belligerent."

"Your father tried to explain, but Aldur wouldn't listen. He called your father a hypocrite. You see, Liesel"—her mother reached over and grasped her daughter's arm—"this attraction Aldur has for Ursula and her politics is about hurting your father. That's why we must be patient with him. We must pray."

~*~*~

His nurse had her hands full in the back autoclaving hypodermic needles, so Juhl left his chart-covered desk to answer the door himself.

"Come in, Eric! Come in! Don't tell me you have another emergency."

Jensen smiled wearily. "How is the Lillelund boy?"

"I'll check on him tonight. If he is strong enough, we will smuggle him into Sweden next week."

"Then you found a fisherman willing to take the risk?"

"Did you doubt that I would?"

Again Jensen smiled. "No, not really."

Juhl waved his colleague to take a seat. "So, tell me," he said as he sat behind his desk, "to what do I owe the honor of your visit?"

Jensen reached into his lab coat, removed a folded sheet of stationary and shoved it across the blotter on Juhl's desk. "Dr. Koster has called for a special meeting at seven tonight. That's his address. Can you make it?"

"What's this meeting about?"

"He is calling it the meeting of the Sixty-Four."

"Ah!" Now Juhl understood.

At the beginning of Denmark's occupation, sixty-four physicians had signed an agreement with the king's policy of negotiation with Berlin. So long as Denmark's Jews retained full citizenship, the Sixty-Four had sworn to cooperate.

Jensen adjusted his glasses. "Now that martial law has been declared, he wants us to form a contingency plan."

"A contingency plan to do what?"

"That's what we'll decided tonight, that and how far we will go if the worst comes to pass."

"Do you think it will?" Juhl asked.

Jensen shrugged. Leaning back in his chair, he removed his glasses and rubbed the bridge of his nose "I never thought it would get this far. The king is a virtual hostage, and Parliament has resigned." Jensen sighed, replaced his spectacles, then sat upright in the chair. "At this point, Juhl, I'm pretty sure it will."

That was not what Juhl wanted to hear, not with his daughter about to marry a Jew—albeit a Christian one. The boy's faith in Christ would be of no consequence to the Nazis. Flem's non-Aryan blood was all Hitler cared about. Craving something cold and wet to remove the foul taste in his mouth, Juhl slipped Dr. Koster's address into his lab coat's breast pocket then went over to his credenza and poured a glass of water. "Would you like some?" he asked Jensen.

"No thanks," he replied. "So, what do you say? Can you make it tonight?"

"I'll be there," Juhl promised. "You can count on it."

~*~*~

Sol Lund let himself in just before noon. Nettie stood at the bottom of the stairs, her arms loaded with folded bath towels.

"What are you doing home so early?" she asked. "Is something wrong?"

Sol slipped off his jacket and hung it on the rack. Not ready to answer her, he took the laundry out of her arms and placed it on the entry table in the foyer, then he took her by the arm and led her into the parlor.

"You're scaring me, Sol. Has something happened? Please tell me Inger has not been hurt."

He sat her on the sofa then sat down next to her. "Rabbi Friediger has been arrested."

Nettie gasped. "Rabbi Friediger? Why?"

"The Reich interned him and some others yesterday. Rabbi Melchior will be filling in for him in the meantime."

Nettie began to weep. "I can't believe this is happening, Sol."

"Be quiet, Nettie, I'm not finished. At 3 a.m. this morning, the Gestapo started banging on the Goldberg's door. Our Cantor and his two older boys are now in hiding."

"How did you find out?"

"I went to his apartment, hoping he could give me some advice about how to handle Flem. Mrs. Hansen, his neighbor, recognized me and pulled me aside. We can thank her for his escape. His wife and his two younger sons had left for the country the day before. That's what gave Mrs. Hansen the idea."

"What idea?"

71

"She knew darn well that at 3 a.m. the Gestapo wasn't there to present them with a key to the city, so, pretending she didn't know who was making all the noise, she yells down the stairwell, 'They left yesterday for a holiday.' "

"And the Gestapo believed her?"

Sol shrugged. "Apparently so. They left, but they posted a guard in front of the building."

"I've been afraid this would happen," his wife said, weeping. "What are we going to do, Sol?"

"After the Gestapo left, the Cantor and his two boys sneaked down the back stairs to the basement. Mrs. Hansen followed them." Sol smiled for the first time. "You'll never guess what the Cantor asked her for."

"What? A gun?"

"A mirror and an electric razor. He shaved off his beard. Then they escaped through an inner courtyard. Hopefully, they made it to the train station without being spotted."

"Where will they go?"

Sol shrugged. "I don't know. His missus and two other boys went to their summerhouse in Rungsted. But he can't go there now, and he can't call to warn them because the Gestapo probably has their phone tapped. So, I don't know, Nettie. I don't know."

Chapter Ten

Flem sat in the boat's cabin, trying not to think about his father's attitude as he helped Katlev mend the last of the nets. He was glad that he'd moved in with the old man. It made him feel independent, like a man about to take on the responsibility of a wife. His only regret was the twenty-minute bike ride that now separated him from Liesel. There would be no more sneaking through his backyard after curfew. But in a few weeks, they would be married. Flem had to be patient.

He ripped off his cap, wiped his brow with his sleeve, then grabbed the last net and tossed it onto the pile with the others. With the piston replaced and the crankcase fixed, he and Katlev would be putting out to sea early the next morning.

Fishing could be exhausting, but he loved the sea, and working with the old man was a treat…and not just because he was so knowledgeable about everything. Katlev was a pleasure to be around, not to mention he was the only one enthusiastic about his upcoming marriage to Liesel. That meant a lot to Flem, especially since his own father and cousin were being so impossible.

"I don't understand him," he told Katlev. "Father has always been so tolerant. It was my mother I always worried about. But now she seems to be coming around. I can't figure them out."

"The Ruach is softening her heart, breaking up the fallow ground. She'll be fine. Just give her time. Her people are from

Denmark, so she wasn't reared on stories of persecution by Christians. Your father was. His people come from Eastern Europe."

"Was it really so bad, Katlev?"

The old man rolled his eyes. "Hellish! And I use the word literally. Christians have committed atrocities against Jews for centuries. They forced Jews to convert at the point of a sword."

"But why?"

"They see us as the assassins of Christ and cursed by God. Do you know how they celebrated Easter during the Middle Ages? They rounded up Jews, shouting, 'Kill a Jew and save your soul.' "

"It's just so hard to believe."

"Well, you can believe it. They also kidnapped Jewish children to baptize them, then murdered their parents. They passed laws that made it illegal for Jews to hold anything but the most menial of jobs. All over Europe we were forced to live in ghettos." Katlev stopped mending his net. "First, we were not allowed to live among them because we were Jews, now Hitler doesn't want us living at all. Even back then, Jews were forced by law to wear badges, and that was centuries before Hitler was born. Where do you think Hitler got his ideas?"

"How could I not have known this?"

Katlev shrugged. "It's history, my boy. Look it up! We've been persecuted for centuries in the name of Christianity."

"It's not what Yeshua teaches. It's not according to the Book."

"The good news is that we didn't have a problem here in Denmark, not until the Nazis occupied us 'to protect us from Churchill,' " Katlev said sarcastically. "It's been quite another story everywhere else, between the Spanish Inquisition and Russia's Pogroms. It didn't start with Hitler. Even men of God, like Martin Luther, fell into Satan's trap."

"Luther? What do you mean?"

Katlev raised an eyebrow. "You don't know about him either?" He shoved aside the net he was mending. "When Luther first broke away from the Roman Church, he went to great lengths to remind his followers that Jesus was a Jew. Of course, he taught that Jesus did away with the Torah, so twenty-some years later, when we Jews had not converted in mass, Luther became furious. He wrote letters to the government. He demanded that rabbis be prohibited from teaching, that our synagogues and homes be torched, and our passports restricted."

No longer able to sit, Flem jumped up.

"Where are you going?" Katlev asked as Flem headed for the steps.

"I need air," he said, wanting to vomit.

~*~*~

Up on deck, Flem hung over the railing as he waited for his stomach to stop churning. Stretching his neck, he drew in a breath of salty air. Praying had helped, only he knew now that he could not marry Liesel, not in a Lutheran church. The Nazis were enforcing the very measures Martin Luther had called for.

It was getting too cold to be on deck without his jacket, and Flem needed to talk to his friend.

"Feeling better?" Katlev asked when Flem entered the cabin.

"A little, but I have a problem, a big problem."

"Well, don't just stand there. Out with it!"

"I can't marry Liesel."

Katlev put down the net he was mending and stared as if stunned.

"Not the way we had planned to," Flem explained. "Not in a Lutheran church."

"Oh, I see..." Katlev said, looking relieved.

"Am I wrong?"

Katlev began stroking his beard. "You must decide that for yourself. You're the one getting married."

"Do you think Pastor Uri resents me? He acted scandalized when I told him I accepted Messiah but would always remain a Jew."

"I can't read hearts, my boy."

"You must have some thoughts on the matter. Come on, Katlev, I need your guidance."

"Scripture is our guidance, Flem. It says we are to judge a tree by its fruit."

"Exactly! That's what I am doing."

"No! You're not!"

"How can you say that?" Flem asked.

"Here in Denmark we Jews have been accepted. More than accepted! We've been welcomed like nowhere else, and these Danes, Flem, are mostly Lutheran!"

Katlev's answer slapped him in the face. But Flem knew it was the truth. Ashamed, he collapsed on the bench across from Katlev. "You're right. You're absolutely right."

Katlev smiled. "I know it is hard, my boy, but you can't let resentment—justified or not—defile your spirit. Remember that Yeshua asked the Father to forgive those crucifying Him. How can we do anything less?"

"But I'm just a man."

"No, Flem, not just a man. You are a man who is being conformed to the Messiah's image."

Flem thought about that for a moment. "You're right. Thanks, Katlev." He got up from the table and gave the old man a hug. "I wonder if Liesel knows about Luther," he said, as he let Katlev go.

"Probably not. Most Christians don't."

"Is it wrong for me to tell her?"

"That all depends on how you go about it."

Flem sighed. "At least I now understand why my father feels the way he does."

"Be patient with him, Flem."

"It isn't easy being conformed, is it?"

"Easy? No. Worth it? Absolutely!"

Flem smiled. "How long have you been conforming, Katlev?"

Sadness flickered in Katlev's eyes. He glanced up at the clock. "It's almost four. You better go if you want to see that girl of yours. It will be curfew before you know it."

Katlev had done it again. Just when Flem thought he was finally about to get the whole story, the old man changed the subject. "I'll see you at your place later," Flem said, snatching his jacket off the hook, determined that tonight he would get some answers.

~*~*~

Exhausted from pacing and peering out her window, Liesel threw herself across her bed. Where was he? Flem should have been there by now. She punched her pillow, but it didn't help. She had to compose herself. She had to stay calm. Crying over something that happened so long ago was insane.

Her parents had worked things out, her father had confessed his sin, and God had forgiven him. It was over! Done with! She couldn't—no, wouldn't—let this drive her crazy like it was driving her brother. Only, if it wasn't over for Aldur, how could it be over for her?

Marinating in her conundrum, Liesel pulled a fresh hanky out of the dresser then returned to the window. Three bicycles passed by, followed by an ice truck, then the elderly couple who lived around the block. But no Flem! Why had he picked this, of all times, to move out of his house? It wasn't fair!

For the third time in an hour, she prayed that Flem would hurry up. Then suddenly he appeared, peddling furiously down her street. She ran to her vanity and was still powdering her face when he knocked at her door.

~*~*~

On his ride from the dock, Flem practiced different ways to tell Liesel about what Katlev had told him about Martin Luther. He was determined to be as gentle as possible, but to tell Liesel the truth, the whole ugly truth. All that changed as soon as Liesel opened the door. Her expression warned him that something was wrong.

"I have to talk to you," she said shutting the door behind her. "Aldur will be home soon, and my father. So, we can't talk inside."

"Let's go to the gazebo."

"I'll get my jacket," she said and darted back into her house.

A minute later, they were crunching on a carpet of dead leaves that led to the Lunds' gazebo. Fall had come early. It was a perfect metaphor for everything that was happening, Flem thought as he brushed away dead foliage from the bench. He motioned Liesel to have a seat.

"You won't believe what I'm about to tell you," she said breathlessly. "And you can't breathe a word of this to anyone."

"Of course," Flem said, as he sat next to her.

"Mother told me why Aldur has been so hateful," she said, then related the conversation she had with her mother. "This whole Nazi business is Aldur's way of getting back at my father. How could he have done it, Flem? My father, I mean?"

Flem shrugged, then put his arm around her. "We all make mistakes, Liesel. When we sow to our flesh, we reap corruption."

"But, he's my father. I needed him to be perfect."

Flem frowned. "Isn't that idolatry?"

"But he's my father!"

"Human beings are fallible. Yeshua has forgiven him, so has your mother. Can you do any less? Sometimes even men of God commit atrocities. It's why we need the Messiah."

"Men of God do not commit atrocities, Flem!"

"Oh, really? What about Martin Luther?"

"What about him?"

"Never mind." Flem wished he had kept his mouth shut.

"You brought it up. Now explain yourself!"

"It's getting really cold out here." Flem pulled her to her feet. "Why don't we go inside?"

"I want to know what you meant."

"I'll tell you later. I promise, but first I need to pray."

"Pray about what?"

Flem took a deep breath. How could he answer that without making matters worse? "About my attitude," he finally said.

"Your attitude? We were talking about Martin Luther."

"Are you trying to pick a fight with me, Liesel?"

She searched his eyes, then sighed. "All right! Let's go inside."

Chapter Eleven

Juhl Prestur got home at six-thirty, exhausted but exhilarated by two emergencies, emergencies that could get him, another doctor, two interns, and five nurses dragged in front of a German firing squad. Their crime? Treating saboteurs! Falsifying charts! Reporting gunshot wounds as appendectomies!

Juhl and all eight of his co-conspirators at Bispebjerg Hospital were happy to do it, and they would be happy to do it all again. Of that, Juhl was certain. From janitors to ambulance drivers, hospital employees had joined forces to help the Resistance. Juhl had witnessed it firsthand. It elated and exhausted him. He would eat and go up to bed if he hadn't already promised to attend that meeting at Dr. Koster's tonight.

As Juhl tossed his hat on the rack, Liesel ran up to him. She took hold of his hands. "I'm so sorry, Father. Can you forgive me?"

"Forgive you for what?" he asked.

"I know why Mother went to visit Aunt Clare."

His daughter's words punched him in the gut. Deidre had promised him they would tell Liesel together, so Aldur must have spilled the beans.

"It's okay, Father. You don't need to look so upset." She stroked his cheek. "I've already forgiven you. Flem made me see reason."

"I'm so sorry, *yndling*. I never wanted you to find out this way. Just know that the pain, the torment I brought on your mother and myself, drove me to my knees. The Lord changed me."

"I know," Liesel said, tearing up.

"He has changed, Liesel," his wife called out from the dining room.

"God healed our marriage," Juhl said as Aldur entered through the front door. "And He has kept our family together."

Aldur scoffed, shaking his head. "What pompous hypocrisy!" he said, as Deidre rushed in from the dining room.

"Apologize to your father this minute, Aldur! Do you hear me? Apologize!"

"I'm sorry," he said without conviction.

"Now go get cleaned up for supper! Well, don't just stand there. Go!"

"I'm not hungry, Mother. I've lost my appetite," he said sneering at Flem.

"What's wrong with you?" Deidre demanded, then snatched Aldur's cap off his head and swatted his shoulder. Aldur turned and staggered toward the stairs.

"Can't you tell what's wrong with him?" Juhl asked. "He smells like a brewery!" Deidre started to go after him, but Juhl stopped her. "Let him go. He needs to sleep it off."

Halfway up, Aldur turned around. "Better be careful, Flem. Keep seeing my sister and Father will baptize you."

"Don't mind him, Flem," Juhl said. "It's just the beer talking."

"He's getting worse, Juhl," Deidre cried. "We have to do something."

"I know, but not tonight. I have a meeting at Dr. Koster's. You and Liesel will be dining alone."

"How late will you be?" his wife asked.

"I don't know, but I need to get ready."

"I better leave too," Flem said, checking his wristwatch.

"I'm sorry for my son's behavior, Flem," Deidre apologized. "We have to keep praying for him."

"Don't worry about it, Mrs. Prestur. I'm not offended."

Noticing Flem's smile, Juhl asked, "Does praying for my son strike you as funny?"

"No! Of course not. I was just wondering what Aldur would've said if I told him I already have been."

"Have been what?" Juhl asked.

"Baptized. Katlev insisted on it. Only, in Hebrew we call it a mikvah."

Juhl smiled. Then everyone started to laugh.

~*~*~

Juhl entered the oak-paneled library and took a seat next to Dr. Koster. "Where is everyone?" he asked, disappointed to find only five at the conference table.

"We're all here, now that you've arrived," Koster replied.

Juhl glanced at Dr. Jensen then back at his host, who was pouring some schnapps. "Forgive my presumption, but I thought this was the meeting of the Sixty-Four."

Koster peered at Juhl over the top his spectacles. "Have you forgotten that large gatherings have been restricted?" He handed the schnapps to Kieler, on his right. "The only reason we six can be here after curfew is because we're all doctors."

"Of course," Juhl said. "Forgive my lapse."

Several doctors smiled. Jensen got up and handed each of them a sheet of paper. "You're all responsible to report what we decide tonight to the doctors on your list."

Juhl scanned the thirteen names on his list as Koster returned to his seat. He poured another tumbler of schnapps, handed it to Juhl, then raised his glass. "To freedom!"

"To freedom!" they all responded.

After Juhl took a sip, he asked the question that had consumed him ever since he learned about their meeting. "So, when do we start smuggling the Jews out of Denmark?"

"Who said anything about that?" Dr. Legarth asked, looking appalled. "We have to move cautiously."

"I'm afraid we won't have that luxury," Juhl replied. "We're already under martial law."

"Juhl's right," Jensen said. "Time is of the essence."

81

"But we've had crackdowns before," Legarth said. "We must use diplomacy."

"Diplomacy?" Juhl said. "You can't be serious."

Legarth leaned forward. "I assure you, Dr. Prestur, I am, and I find your tone condescending."

"All right, gentlemen, calm down," Koster said. "Let's not get our blood pressure up. We are all here because we want to help."

Tempering his ire with schnapps, Juhl drained his tumbler and set it down. "Forgive me, Dr. Legarth. I don't doubt your good intentions, only the efficacy of using diplomacy with Nazis. Such a plan would—"

"Plan? What plan?" Legarth bellowed. "We haven't even formed a plan yet."

"What difference does it make?" Juhl asked. "Any plan that depends on diplomacy with the Reich will fail."

Legarth's face turned red. "You're a hothead! That's what you are. A hothead!"

"Gentlemen, please," Koster begged. "Let's not call each other names. We're colleagues not adversaries. Now go on, Juhl. Make your point."

Juhl took a deep breath. Somehow, he had to make them understand. Lives depended on it. "Diplomacy only works when the parties involved not only compromise but stick to their bargain. I can assure you, Hitler will not! Or have you forgotten our non-aggression treaty?"

"Of course, I haven't," Legarth said. "But need I remind you that Jews here are not wearing yellow stars, nor are they living in ghettos?"

"They will be!" Juhl said. "Or worse."

"Not if we make it clear to the Germans that we won't stand for it," Legarth countered.

"And how do you propose we do that?" Juhl asked.

Legarth glared. "You're being condescending again, Doctor!"

"How can I make you understand?" Juhl asked. "Nazis can't be trusted!"

"Stop it, both of you!" Koster pounded his gavel. "I won't have this! Do you hear?"

Everyone grew silent.

Finally, Jensen posed a suggestion. "What if we approach every civic and economic group in Denmark, the Chamber of Commerce, unions, industrial and agricultural boards, and ask them to write letters to Werner Best demanding no action be taken against the Jews?"

Juhl felt his blood pressure rising. "Or what? What exactly are we willing to do? That's what I want to know."

"It might be best to keep it allusive," Jensen suggested. "Let them imagine the worst."

"It's worth a try," Koster agreed.

Juhl had to bite his tongue. Reasoning with fools was like spitting against the wind. Sooner or later, they would have to formulate a real plan. He just hoped there would be time to do it. His only daughter was about to marry a Jew.

~*~*~

Leaving out the salacious parts regarding his soon-to-be father-in-law's indiscretions, Flem unburdened himself to Katlev about his tumultuous afternoon with Liesel. They finished the dishes and went into the parlor. Now it was time to wheedle out of the old man his reason for avoiding talking about his epiphany.

"Every time I've asked you to tell me about how you came to faith in Yeshua you've put me off. Why?"

"Have I?" Katlev asked, avoiding eye contact.

"Why don't you want to talk about it?"

Katlev sighed. "I was twenty-four when Yeshua saved me."

"You've served Him for fifty years?"

"I wouldn't call it serving exactly." Katlev sat in his favorite chair. "Ran is more like it. Feeling like Peter must have felt after denying the Lord, I did what Peter did. I went fishing."

"Why didn't you become a rabbi?"

"I wasn't worthy. I was a coward."

That was hard to believe. "Was it because of Yeshua?"

Katlev stared into the fireplace. "There were three of us, three best friends, Jacob Mitzger, Matityahu Goldberg, and me. The three Musketeers—all for one and one for all—since childhood. After graduating from the university, we all felt called to become rabbis."

It was difficult to picture Katlev as a child, and harder still to think of him as a coward. Flem leaned forward. "Here in Copenhagen?"

"In Germany."

"You're a German Jew?"

"It's not something I like talking about," Katlev said, examining one of his fingernails.

"Well, if you would rather not talk about it," Flem said, feeling his friend's discomfort, "you don't have to."

Katlev looked him in the eye. "You should know this, Flem. I don't want you to ever make my mistake."

"Well, if you are sure."

"While we were in the *yeshiva*, Jacob started seeing a young lady named Sima. She was a beauty. Her father was a prominent rabbi, active in the Zionist movement. Jacob was crazy about her. An opportunity arose for Sima to spend a summer in Jerusalem with some cousins, so, naturally, she took it. Jacob was happy for her, but miserable for himself, and so were we."

Flem smiled. "All for one and one for all."

Katlev nodded sadly. "That was the beginning of the end."

"What do you mean?"

"Of life as we had known it." Once more Katlev gazed at the flames in the fireplace. "Sima left us the dutiful daughter of a respected rabbi. Three months later, she returned as a scandalous woman."

"What happened?" Flem asked, fearing the worst.

"She came back a disciple of Yeshua."

"What! How did that happen?"

"She met some missionaries."

"How on earth did her cousins allow that?"

Katlev smiled. "They didn't. But the Most High had a plan," he said, then went on to explain that one day when Sima went out for her walk, she was bitten by a snake. "She was delirious by the time some Presbyterians found her. One of them, a retired British Army doctor, recognized her symptoms and brought her back to their camp, where they nursed her through her delirium."

"And witnessed to her about the Messiah?"

Katlev shook his head. "There was no need to. The nurses had read to her from the New Testament while she was delirious. The first word Sima spoke was Jesus."

"God's word penetrated her unconsciousness?"

"It saved the daughter of a rabbi," Katlev said. "Before taking her back to her cousins, they gave her a Bible."

"What did her cousins say about that?"

"They only knew that the missionaries had saved her life. She hid her Bible—and her trips—to go visit with them."

Flem grinned, imagining what his own father's reaction would have been.

"She knew if they ever found out she believed in Jesus they'd book her passage on the first steamer sailing for the continent. And that's exactly what they did. A few weeks later, they packed her off to Germany."

"How did they find out?"

"One of her cousins got suspicious one day and followed her." Katlev rolled his eyes. "Two days later, Sima's trunks were packed. She was driven to the dock and booked on a ship bound for Italy with a one-way train ticket for Berlin in her purse."

"What a testimony!"

"When Jacob heard about what had happened, he was heartsick. He was studying to be a rabbi. How could he marry the love of his life now? He was miserable, and so were we."

"The Three Musketeers…"

"Hoping to talk Sima out of what I thought was a bunch of foolishness, I took it upon myself to prove that Jesus was a fraud. So, I bought a Christian Bible."

"But instead you were convinced."

"It took six months, but yes. Little by little, as I compared passages from the Torah and the Prophets with accounts in the Gospels, HaShem opened my eyes. I could no longer deny it, but I did, just like Peter." The old man gave a gut-wrenching sob.

"If you'd rather not continue, I understand."

Katlev pulled out his handkerchief and blew his nose. "No, I need to finish. I wanted to be a hero and make Sima see the truth. How was I to know I would be the one seeing the light?" He paused for several seconds. "So many times I wanted to go to Jacob and share what God had shown me, but I never got up the nerve. So instead of confiding in Jacob, I went to talk to Sima. She, of course, was elated and begged me to go with her to speak to Jacob. Finally, I agreed."

"What did Jacob say?"

"Sima was so distraught when I stood her up that she never saw the buggy coming. The horses trampled her to death." Tears rolled down the old fisherman's face into his whiskers. "I dropped out of *yeshiva* after that, and never spoke to Jacob again. How could I? How could I tell him I was responsible for her death?"

"It was an accident, Katlev."

"An accident that never would have happened if I had been a man of my word, a man of faith," he said, staring into Flem's eyes. "I left Germany shortly after that, came here and began to fish."

"Yeshua has forgiven you."

"I can't forgive myself. Besides, the story doesn't end there. Seven years later, with the help of a private detective, Matityahu found me. It seems he'd had the same idea I had, and he came to the same conclusion."

"He's a believer, too?"

"By the time he realized Yeshua was the Messiah, he had already become a rabbi."

"That's wonderful!"

"He lost his congregation, and his wife almost left him. When she finally came around to his way of seeing things, they emigrated to Palestine. And guess who they ran into? The Scottish physician who treated Sima's snakebite."

Flem leaned forward, feeling like he was on a rollercoaster, hanging on for dear life.

"The doctor told Matityahu that after Sima left, he and the others continued to pray for her. They prayed that God would use Sima to draw many Jews to Yeshua."

Flem's heart filled with awe. "Those prayers didn't go unanswered, Katlev."

Katlev smiled. "I know. That's when Matityahu decided to hire a private investigator to find me. And he did. Naturally, I told him the truth about Sima, and why I left Germany."

"What about Jacob?"

The old man's smile faded. "He became a rabbi, too...and a bitter man, according to Matityahu. He'd lost the woman he loved, me, and to his way of thinking, Matityahu."

"So, Matityahu never convinced him about Yeshua?"

"He was blinded by pain, but we pray for him still."

"Did he ever leave Germany?"

"Before Hitler came to power?" Katlev shrugged. "I don't know, but with Elohim all things are possible. He reached Sima when she was delirious. Who's to say He won't reach Jacob. Matityahu confronted him with the truth. Now, it's between Jacob and the Lord." He sighed. "I just wonder how differently things might have turned out had I kept my appointment with Sima that day."

Chapter Twelve

08 September, 1943

It was a week since the Danish Government had resigned, and Werner Best was tired of being second in command under General von Hannecken. Now he must act. He grabbed his fountain pen, took out his pad, and wrote: In accordance with Berlin's latest policy regarding Denmark, we will immediately begin to eliminate our Jewish problem. We, therefore, request that you send additional police forces.

Best set down his pen and read over what he had written. Satisfied with its content, he instructed his secretary to telegraph it to Berlin immediately. The telegram, he hoped, would soon restore him to his former position, and his old nemesis, General von Hannecken, would no longer be calling the shots.

Less than twenty-four hours later, Best received the reply he'd been hoping for: "The Reich's foreign minister requests that you submit a complete proposal in order to determine the number of S.S. troops you will require."

The first domino had tumbled. Three days later, on September 11th, 1943, Best decided it was time to break the news to the head of German shipping. He pushed the button on his intercom. "Get Duckwitz on the phone," he told his secretary. "Tell him to come to my office, I need to speak to him right away."

"Certainly, Herr Best."

Twenty minutes later, he informed Duckwitz of Berlin's plan. "We're to round up the Jews in a raid at midnight and deport them to a concentration camp forty miles from Prague."

Duckwitz turned purple. He jumped out of his chair and leaned across Best's desk. "You can't go through with this! You must stop it!'

"I can't! It's too late. Look, I know how you feel, George, but Berlin is in control."

"You must make them see reason!"

Best was losing his patience. "I wish I had that kind of power, George, but I don't!"

"You've convinced them before," George insisted.

"Well, we're in a new season—the Resistance is now out of control."

"Jews aren't!"

"You don't know that!"

"I know the names of the saboteurs that have been arrested," Duckwitz said. "Not one of them is Jewish!"

"That only proves how crafty they are, not their innocence."

"Now you sound like Goebbels!"

That did it. Best pounded his desk. "What do you expect me to do, George? Refuse the Führer?"

Duckwitz glared right back at him. "I expect you to show leadership, to act like the man you once were."

"Well, I am sorry to have to disappoint you, but things have changed."

"Not as sorry as I am!" George said. He clicked his heels and stormed out of Best's office, not bothering to give the salute, which infuriated Best even more.

Trying to calm down, Best paced the floor, brooding. But instead of feeling better, an ominous foreboding washed over him. He pulled out his cigarette case for a smoke. What in God's name had he started?

~*~*~

Two hours later, George's telephone rang. Since the communications ban was still in effect, he knew it had to be from Headquarters. George picked up the receiver.

"I must talk to you right away!" Werner Best said.

George bristled. "About what?"

"Not over the telephone," Best said, sounding anxious but no longer angry. "Can you come to my office right away?"

Wondering what had caused Best's sudden change in attitude, George said, "I'm on my way."

Twenty minutes later, when George entered Best's office, Best greeted him with a smile. He rushed to George's side, offering his hand instead of the usual salute. "How about a little schnapps?"

George shrugged. "If you insist," he said and took a seat.

"I don't usually drink this early in the day, but with so much going on I figured we could both use a little fortification."

"Why did you summon me?"

"We've been friends for a long time, George." Best poured a second tumbler. "I felt terrible about the way our conversation ended earlier. I just wanted to clear the air between us."

"Will you try to dissuade Berlin?"

Best raised one of the tumblers to his lips and drained it. "It's too late, George. I sent Ribbentrop a cable before you came by earlier. I told him how many S.S. we will need," he said, handing George his schnapps. "There's no turning back now, I'm afraid."

"Then why am I here?"

"To let you know how bad I feel."

"I see," George said. He stood and handed the schnapps back to Best. "You need this more than I do." Tomorrow George would fly to Berlin.

~*~*~

Preparing for bed, Liesel sat at her vanity, brushing her hair as she reflected on everything that had happened. The Reich had pushed curfew back to 8 p.m. Her father had procured a part-time job for her in the hospital's business office. Katlev had opened his home to Flem and to her, once she and Flem were married.

Most of all, Liesel was grateful to the Lord for softening her soon-to-be mother-in-law's heart. Flem's father was a different story. He grew more distant each passing day. As for Inger, Liesel thought, with a heavy sigh as she laid down her brush, the girl remained a challenge. But God was working on Inger, too. Liesel was sure of it. And miracle of miracles, since the night her brother had come home drunk, he had left her alone.

In Copenhagen, King Christian had stopped making his daily horseback rides through the city. Tension was high. All over town, Danes had started wearing red, white, and blue stocking caps to show their allegiance with Britain. Ribbons of red and white, Denmark's colors, were in vogue on jackets and sweaters everywhere. At the end of the ribbons, Danes tied four coins that equaled a value of nine, their coded protest for April 9th, the date on which Nazis had descended upon them three years earlier.

Liesel opened her jewelry box and took out her protest ribbon. Her future in Denmark as Mrs. Fleming Lund didn't look promising. Perhaps she should go with Flem and Katlev when they smuggled Sven Lillelund into Sweden and not come back. Sven would be well enough to leave in a few more days.

Excited by that possibility, Liesel climbed into bed, determined to present her plan to Flem the next day.

~*~*~

13 September, 1943

A heaviness George Duckwitz had never known before crushed him as he boarded the airplane back to Denmark. His mission to the Foreign Ministry Office in Berlin had been a colossal waste of time. Werner Best had been right. There was no turning back now. Ribbentrop had already forwarded Best's telegram to the Führer, who had ordered Heinrich Himmler to follow through with the logistics. Soon representatives from Adolf Eichmann's Jewish

Affairs Office would be dispatched to Copenhagen, along with troops, trucks, and transport ships. Save a miracle of biblical proportions, all of Denmark's 7,500 Jews were destined for Theresienstadt Concentration Camp.

That left only one thing that George could do.

Chapter Thirteen

From the moment Liesel flung open the front door, Flem could see her excitement. Her blue eyes gleamed as static electricity lifted several strands of her otherwise silky hair.

"We have to talk!"

"Don't we always?" Flem asked, trying not to laugh.

"In private," she said, glancing over her shoulder.

"Then get your jacket," he said.

She dashed back in, leaving the front door open. Flem stepped in and shut the door, just as Aldur came bounding down the stairs.

"Out of my way!" he said.

Flem stepped aside, then on impulse, he clasped Aldur's arm as he passed. "Look, I don't know what I've done to offend you, but whatever it is, I'm sorry."

Aldur glared at Flem's hand.

Flem let him go.

"Your very presence offends me!" Aldur told him.

"That's enough!" Liesel said, jumping between them. "You had better remember what Father told you. Your insane hatred must stop! Now apologize!"

Aldur sneered. "It's not hatred to remove vermin from one's home!"

"Flem isn't vermin! This is my home too, Aldur. So, stop parroting your indecent propaganda!"

Dr. Prestur rushed down the hall. "That's enough, both of you!"

Mrs. Prestur followed close behind. Flem had never seen her so pale. Why had he not kept his mouth shut?

"Didn't you hear what Aldur said?" Liesel asked her father.

"It turned my stomach!" Dr. Prestur said, glaring at his son. "One more crack like that and I'll toss you out on your ear. Do you hear me?"

"Juhl, please!" Mrs. Prestur said. "Let's not make things worse."

"Forget it, Mother! Father has wanted my absence for some time now."

"That is not true," his mother cried. "Tell him, Juhl! Tell him!"

Dr. Prestur said nothing.

"Well, Mother, there is your answer. And don't let him try to convince you that this has anything to do with my politics. It's his guilt."

The vein on Dr. Prestur's temple pulsed wildly. He drew back his arm and punched Aldur's jaw. Mrs. Prestur screamed as her son staggered backward. Recovering quickly, Aldur balled his fist, ready to return the blow. But Liesel and her mother grabbed his arm and restrained him.

Aldur shook them off. "The sooner I am out of here the better. I'm going up to pack."

"I am so sorry," Flem said once Aldur had left the room. "It's my fault. I never should have tried to engage him, not without praying first."

"It's not you, Flem," Dr. Prestur said. "I sowed these seeds, and now I am reaping my harvest."

"No, Juhl! Our son must bear some of the responsibility."

"Flem and Liesel should not have to go through this. Not in our home," he told her.

"It's okay, Dr. Prestur. It could have been worse."

"Well, if the rumors I'm hearing are true, things are about to get worse," Dr. Prestur said. "Much worse."

"What have you heard, Father?"

"There's been talk about deporting the Jews."

"Such rumors have spread before," Mrs. Prestur reminded them.

They all grew silent. Then Flem took Liesel outside to his parents' gazebo. "I should have kept my mouth shut," he said as he cleared leaves from the bench.

"My brother wanted this to happen, Flem. It proves, to him at least, what a rogue my father is. But forget Aldur!" She took hold of Flem's hand. "I have something I must talk to you about."

"Go on. I'm listening."

"Father thinks Sven will be able to leave the parsonage in a few days."

"Wonderful! Katlev's been itching to make the trip. He plans on offering his services to the Resistance after his maiden voyage."

"The Resistance? Flem, that's so dangerous!"

Flem tipped up her chin. "We are Jews, my love. We're in jeopardy one way or another. Besides, Katlev is convinced that Yeshua sent him to Copenhagen for this very purpose." Flem then went on to tell her about the three Musketeers. He ended with Rabbi Matityahu's visit seven years later.

"Katlev believes that his smuggling Sven to Sweden will be a transitional voyage from exile to purpose."

"What you don't understand is that I want to go, too."

"Absolutely not! That's out of the question!"

"I want us—you and me—to escape to Sweden."

~*~*~

Flem didn't sleep that night. He tossed and turned and had a nightmare. In it, he and some friends he'd grown up with were mowed down by a German firing squad.

The next morning, while they were putting out to sea, Flem turned to Katlev. "Liesel asked me to stay in Sweden with her when we take Sven."

The old man looked worried. "What did you tell her?"

"That it's out of the question. But then she wore me down. I promised her I would pray about it."

"Have you gotten an answer?"

"Just now…and a release."

"Oh, I see…"

"No! I don't think you do. I'm staying here with you. Elohim wants me to. I can't run away from this any more than you can."

~*~*~

Sol Lund donned his overcoat, desperate to talk to someone who would understand how he felt. He grabbed his hat off the rack and informed his secretary that he had something he must do and would see her on Monday. Outside, as he made his way down the street, his feet felt heavy, as if they were made of cement. The smell of burning leaves filled the air. It was a scent he'd always loved. But today, it was just smoke in his nose. Two women greeted him as he approached the bus stop. Sol tipped his hat, without returning their smile. It was the best he could do.

He checked his pocket watch. If it was accurate, his bus should be turning the corner any minute. The pocket watch had been a birthday gift from Flem. Sol sighed, placing it back in his pocket. What a time for the boy, who all his life had been such a blessing, to start giving him such heartache. Sol swallowed hard, forcing his mind to go blank in an effort to stave off any tears.

Thirty seconds later, his bus arrived. Sol took a seat all the way in back where many were still empty. Shimon Kodet was the only man he wanted to talk to, the only man who might be able to advise him. Shimon had suffered a similar problem with his recalcitrant daughter.

When the bus stopped in front of the Jewish Center, Sol got off, relieved there were no German soldiers posted outside. But how long would that last? When would *Kristallnacht*—the night of broken glass—begin in Denmark? When would jackbooted storm troopers rampage through Copenhagen, demolishing everything Jewish? If his son, his only son, could become a Lutheran, anything was possible.

Inside, the Jewish Center was empty except for two old men playing chess. Then Sol spotted Shimon sitting against the back wall reading a newspaper.

"What's this?" Shimon asked. "Is the headmaster skipping school?"

"I'm running away. Care to join me?"

"If I could get a visa, I'd leave with my whole family. I might even take my wife's brother if that tells you anything."

Sol pulled up a chair next to him. Shimon folded his paper and shoved it aside. "I don't know why I even bother reading that fish-wrapper anymore."

Sol nodded his agreement.

"Seriously," Shimon said. "What brings you here? You look terrible."

"Is there somewhere we can talk? I don't want to be overheard."

"No need to worry about those two. They're practically deaf," Shimon assured him. "If I turn up the radio, they won't hear a word." He got up, tuned the station to a dance band, then returned to his seat. "What's on your mind, my friend?"

"It's my son."

"Don't tell me he's been arrested."

"He's become a Lutheran."

"A Lutheran?"

Cringing at Shimon's volume, Sol glanced over his shoulder. The two old men remained engrossed in their game. "My son thinks that calling his new Christian god by a Hebrew name makes everything okay, *kol b'seder*."

"Come again?"

"This crazy old fisherman that my son's been working for has filled Flem's head with all sorts of heresies."

"Oh, I see…"

"On top of that, Flem wants to marry the girl next door—the Lutheran girl next door."

"*Oy gevalt.*"

"*Oy gevalt*, indeed!" Sol said. "He wants to quit school and work full time for that *mishuga* so he can marry the girl." Sol shrugged. "I don't know what to do."

"You certainly have trouble."

"Things can't get any worse!" Sol said as both front doors flew open.

Four German S.S. officers entered the Jewish Community Center with the center's librarian in tow. Like a trapped animal, the librarian's eyes were dilated by fear.

"This establishment is now closed," one of the soldiers announced.

"They've come for our membership records," the terrified librarian explained. "You must all go home now."

Chapter Fourteen

When Foreign Minister Nils Svenningsen found out the S.S. had shut down the Jewish Community Center, he barged into Werner Best's office at the Embassy, barely pausing long enough to apologize to Best's secretary for the intrusion.

"The untenable has finally happened," Nils said. "You must do something!"

Best waved his secretary out of the room.

"Please, have a seat."

"I prefer to stand."

"May I pour you a drink?"

"The Jewish Community Center was just broken into. I want answers, Werner, and they better be the right ones. Records containing the addresses of their members were seized. I demand to know why!"

Best folded his arms. "If my memory serves me correctly, your government has resigned. Berlin is now in control."

"We won't allow you to persecute our Jews!"

"Calm yourself, Nils. It was a routine search for saboteurs."

"You expect me to believe that?"

"I do." Best replied without flinching.

Nils began to relax. Perhaps he was overreacting. But who wouldn't with so many rumors swirling? Copenhagen was holding its breath, just waiting for the next shoe to fall.

"If you can assure me this is not the beginning of a round up, I will consider the matter closed, but I can't attest for the others."

"The others? What others?"

"Hans Hedtof for one. We were having lunch when we learned of the incident."

"Oh, I see," Best said.

Nils toyed with pointing out that the meal had been a working lunch held at the Democratic Party Headquarters, with all members present, but he decided not to. If Best was telling him the truth—and for the Jews' sake, he prayed Best was—then this visit was an overreaction.

~*~*~

Best poured himself another drink the minute Nils Svenningsen left his office. Since George was the head of German shipping, he would have to be told the truth, the whole truth.

Best drained his schnapps and left his office.

George's secretary glanced up from her typewriter when Best entered the shipping office. "How good to see you." She reached for the intercom. "I'll let Herr Duckwitz know you're here."

"I prefer to surprise him. Just see that we're not disturbed."

George didn't look up from the document he was pouring over until Best cleared his throat. "Heil Hitler."

"Heil Hitler," George replied.

"I was just paid a visit by the foreign minister. He wanted to take my head off. I calmed him down, of course. I'm getting rather good at that."

"Why was he upset?"

"Eichmann's commandos arrived this morning, and a couple of them paid a visit to the Jewish Community Center."

"They did what?"

"Berlin is pulling all the strings now, George. I had nothing to do with it. I'm merely the plenipotentiary."

"What did they want?" George asked, fumbling with his cigarette case.

"A list of addresses." Noting George's expression, Best added, "You must stop letting this eat you up, George. It's out of our hands. The date has been set. On September 29th, transport ships will dock in this harbor, and at midnight, October 1st, the raid will begin."

"But the first is Rosh Hashanah!"

Best shrugged. "Of course, and all the Jews will be at home."

~*~*~

By now, most everyone in Copenhagen had heard that the Reich had confiscated a list of Jewish addresses. They were scared because most everyone had someone, a relative, a co-worker, or a friend, who was Jewish.

For Juhl Prestur that fear was mixed with guilt. Theologically, he knew he was forgiven, only that didn't undo the consequence—the law of cause and effect. He assuaged his guilt for having turned his son into a Nazi by taking greater risks. Through aiding the Resistance, Juhl hoped he could balance the scales.

So, two days before Flem and Katlev were scheduled to smuggle the Lillelund boy across the Sound, Juhl proposed a change to their plan. Juhl would drive Sven, disguised as a girl, further up the coast outside of Elsinore, where the distance between Denmark and Sweden was only four kilometers. There, he and Sven would rendezvous, at sunset, with Flem and Katlev.

~*~*~

The night of the rendezvous was cloudy. The moon was no more than a sliver. The rowboat would be quieter, thus safer than Katlev's cutter. "Just remember to listen for patrol boats," Juhl whispered as the vessel pulled away from shore.

"We will," Katlev called back. "The Most High will guide us."

He'll have to, Juhl thought, waving. The Germans sometimes turned off their motors. He patted his pocket, making sure his tiny flashlight was still in it. He would need it to give them the signal when they returned. Then the three of them would spend what was left of the night aboard Katlev's cutter. In the morning, he would drive back to Copenhagen alone.

Remembering that the book he brought to read was still in the glove compartment, he hurried back to the boathouse and retrieved it. Halfway back to the pier where Katlev had docked his boat, Juhl heard a man whisper in English, "Over here, mate."

Juhl stopped and looked around.

"I need help. Me leg's busted."

"Where are you?" Juhl asked, scanning the beach.

"About twenty paces to your left. I'm in the brush."

Juhl stared in that direction. As his eyes adjusted to the dark, he began to make out a silhouette. Shoving his book in his pocket, he glanced around. No one was watching. When he reached the man's side, Juhl knelt next to him. "Which leg is it? I'm a doctor."

"My right."

Juhl pushed his thumb through a tear in the Brit's pant leg and ripped it to the hem. Then he turned on his flashlight. The leg was swollen below the knee cap. But as best as he could tell, neither the tibia nor the fibula had pierced the man's skin.

"Can you stand on your good leg?"

"If I had a crutch."

Juhl pulled the man to his feet. "Put your arm around me. We're going to that pier over there. I need to get you into the boat."

"The Germans will be making another pass soon."

"Are you sure?"

"They've been patrolling this area every forty-five minutes."

"Are you a pilot?" Juhl asked as they trudged down the beach.

"Gunnery sergeant, Royal Air Force. Tyler Tamree is the name. We bailed out before running out of fuel. I don't know what's happened to the rest of my crew. I must have drifted farther north."

"Where's your parachute?" Juhl asked.

"Buried in the brush."

As they made their way to the boat, Juhl began to pray. This would certainly complicate his plans, but he had no choice. He had to trust God and keep walking.

When they reached the pier, Juhl set the gunnery sergeant down on the dock and jumped into the cutter.

Tyler scooted his bottom to the edge of the pier and Juhl opened his arms. "Ready to jump?"

"As ready as I'll ever be."

"Bend that knee. You don't want that foot to hit the deck."

"Roger that!"

Tyler shoved off and landed on his good leg, stumbling forward. But Juhl steadied him. They had just reached the cabin when the sound of a motorboat became audible. Both men froze.

As the German patrol boat came alongside of Katlev's cutter, Juhl held his breath.

The German's turned off the motor. "*Ist jemand an Bord? Kennzeichnen Sie sich!*"

"What did he say?" Tyler whispered.

"He's asking if anyone is aboard."

Light filtered through the hatch into the cabin. The Brit drew his weapon.

"*Gehen Sie an Bord und suchen Sie es.*"

"*Es gibt keine dort. Lassen Sie uns gehen.*"

"Now what are they saying?" Tyler asked.

"One of them wants to search the boat. The other one thinks it's unnecessary."

Half a minute passed. Then the patrol boat's motor started up again. Juhl waited for its hum to grow fainter before he dug out his flashlight and searched the wall for a switch. Under sixty watts of brightness, Juhl took his first really good look at his patient's leg.

The gunnery sergeant's eyes glazed with agony.

"Your leg will feel somewhat better once I splint it."

"Do you have something for the pain?"

"Only aspirin. Morphine will make you too woozy. You need to stay alert in case the Germans return."

"I have to find my crew."

"I can put out some feelers come daylight," Juhl said.

"What's your name, Doc?"

"Juhl Prestur. Now I need to turn off the light while I go back to get my bag."

"I'm not afraid of the dark."

Juhl smiled. With only moonlight to guide him, he made his way back to the boathouse, praying that he'd think of a way to get word to the Underground, and that they'd be able to provide sanctuary to the Brit and reunite him with his squadron.

Ten minutes later, with his medical bag in hand, Juhl returned to the cutter and switched on the light. The Brit's eyelids fluttered but never opened. Juhl didn't have the heart to wake him. Sleep was an analgesic too.

He dropped his bag, pulled out his flashlight, then returned to the deck in search of wood to splint that leg. He spotted some crates near the wheelhouse, grabbed one and started looking for a hammer. Finding one, he returned to the cabin and dismantled the crate.

His banging woke up his patient, so Juhl stopped what he was doing and gave him two aspirin. "Do you need something to drink, or can you swallow these dry?"

"I can if I can work up some spit," the gunnery sergeant said, shifting his position. "But water would sure be lovely."

Juhl looked around. Spotting the coffee percolator on the stove gave him hope. Katlev had to store water somewhere. Then Juhl noticed the ice chest. When he lifted its lid there wasn't much ice, but there was a jug of water. Juhl poured some. "Are you hungry?"

"Famished is more like it!"

"I'll see what Katlev has around here to eat. I'm sure he won't mind," Juhl said, opening and closing cupboards. "How about a tin of sardines?"

"I'll have my solicitor name you in my will."

Juhl smiled. "My reward will be in heaven."

"You sound like me mum. Poor as a church mouse, but she never turned away a stranger. She was always casting her bread upon the water."

"You said 'was.' "

"She went on to her reward three years ago."

"I'm sorry," Juhl said, handing the man a tin of sardines. Then

104

he grabbed his hammer and went back to dismantling the crate. With a few good whacks, he freed the piece of wood he needed to splint the leg. After stabilizing it, Juhl turned off the light. In the dark, they waited for the German patrol boat to return.

Chapter Fifteen

Much to Juhl's relief, the boat passed them by, this time without stopping. He turned on the light. "How's the leg?"

"No worse than before. The aspirin helped some, but I could sure use a pillow for my neck."

"Roll up your jacket," Juhl suggested.

"And freeze? I can't get warm as it is."

Juhl felt the sergeant's forehead. "You've got a fever." That wasn't a good sign, Juhl thought as he opened his medical bag, especially since he'd already given him aspirin. "Are you allergic to sulfa or penicillin?"

"Not that I know of," the sergeant said as Juhl shook down his thermometer. The sergeant opened his mouth and Juhl slipped it under his tongue then pulled out his blood pressure cuff.

"Should I make out a will?" the sergeant asked with the thermometer still in his mouth.

Juhl smiled and removed it. "I thought you had one."

"Seriously, Doc, how bad am I?"

"I'm going to give you some penicillin." Jul reached back into his bag for a syringe. He drew up the dose and administered it. "I want you to stay hydrated, so keep drinking water. I can give you more aspirin in a couple of hours. Now try to get some rest. I am going up on deck to look around for a blanket and something you can put under your head.

"You're a good man, Doc."

A few minutes later, Juhl returned with his arms full. "I found you a pillow that smells like fish and a tarp you can use as a blanket."

"Bless you," the sergeant said, slipping the pillow under his head. Juhl covered him with the makeshift blanket.

"Now try to sleep. I won't wake you again unless we get company."

"Then you better take this." The sergeant handed Juhl his weapon. "Have you ever used one before?"

"It's been a while, but I'm sure I can manage."

Juhl flipped off the light, then turned on his flashlight. He made his way to the table, sat down, and began to pray. He was still praying when he heard the hum of the German patrol boat in the distance. He held his breath, and it passed by without stopping.

Juhl turned on the flashlight and checked his watch. Flem and Katlev were due to return in thirty minutes. If they arrived as scheduled, it would give them exactly fifteen minutes to hide the rowboat and make it back to the cutter before the patrol boat returned.

~*~*~

Unable to sleep, Aldur rolled out of bed. He switched on the lamp, grabbed his trousers off the back of a chair and pulled them on. Hoping he wasn't out of cigarettes, he reached into his pockets. Finding a crumpled pack of four, he lit one, then went to the window and looked out.

The streetlight gave off a yellow glow in the fog. Aldur could barely see the street. The authorities would have their hands full tonight. In this soup, there was no telling what the Resistance might be up to, Aldur thought, taking another drag. They were criminals who deserved everything the Reich had in store for them.

Someone tapped on his door. Thinking it was Ursula, Aldur opened it. "Mr. Grund!"

"Did I wake you?"

"No. No, of course not," Aldur said.

"Good! Put on your shirt and come down. We have something to celebrate."

A few minutes later, Mr. Grund handed him a glass of port, then poured one for himself.

"What are we celebrating?" Aldur asked as they sat in front of the fireplace.

"A friend has informed me, and he is very well connected, that we are about to round up the Jews."

"Well, I've heard that before."

"No, no, no! This time it will happen. I assure you."

Aldur sipped his wine. "Did your friend say when?"

"No. But I am sure it will be soon. What purpose would it serve to wait? I haven't been this excited since meeting Goebbels."

"When was that?"

"In 1933, in Berlin. I was visiting a professor friend at Wilhelm Humboldt University, watching history in the making, right there on Franz Joseph Platz."

"History? What do you mean?"

"Germany was purging itself of poisonous lies penned by vermin. We were burning books."

"Written by Jews?"

"Mostly," Mr. Grund said. "But others too. We hauled thousands to the bonfire, singing songs. Goebbels speech was glorious. Believe me, the world took notice, and other universities followed suit. All over Germany, we burned books by radicals, vermin like Freud, Einstein, Hemingway, Dickens, and London."

"Jack London?" Aldur was shocked. "Jack London is not a Jew."

"Perhaps not, but he must have written lies. Goebbels said, 'The future German will not be a man of just books but a man of character.'"

Aldur sipped his port, recalling something he'd read once, something written by a poet whose name escaped him: When one burns books, one soon will burn people.

Miracle Across the Sound

An eerie mist blanketed the Sound. On the shore, in front of the boathouse, Juhl gave the signal a second time and shut off the flashlight. Where were they? They should've returned by now. That German patrol boat would be making its rounds in less than fifteen minutes. The fog must be delaying them. Or worse, something had gone wrong.

The rising tide made the water choppy. Cold permeated Juhl's bones. He checked his watch. In three minutes, he would give the signal one last time. After that, he would have no choice but to take cover in the boathouse.

Starting at 180, he counted down the seconds, then turned on the torch and gave the signal. This time, it was returned. A second later, Juhl heard a boat's motor in the distance and the rhythmic swishing of water.

He shined his torch. Dead ahead he spotted them. "Hurry! There is a German patrol boat coming. We have to hide in the boathouse."

They carried the rowboat inside and shut the door. Outside, the hum of a motor grew louder, then cut off.

"Why are they stopping?" Flem whispered.

"I don't know. But they boarded the cutter earlier and scared us to death."

"Us?" Katlev whispered.

"I'll explain later," Juhl said, opening the door a crack. A spotlight swept the boathouse. Heart hammering, Juhl shut the door.

But the spotlight did not return. Seconds later, the motor kicked back on, then gradually grew fainter.

Juhl opened the door to the boathouse again. "I was afraid they'd found the Brit and had come to hunt us down."

"What Brit?" Flem asked.

"He has a broken leg. I left him sleeping on your boat. Come on," Juhl said, waving them to follow.

Flem fought back a yawn. It was late. The boat was freezing, and they still didn't know what to do with their guest.

"I could try to sneak him into the hospital under an assumed name," Dr. Prestur suggested. "For a few days, at least."

"What about Pastor Uri's place?" Flem suggested.

"That might be easier to pull off," Dr. Prestur admitted. "But he will need a wheelchair."

Katlev glanced at the gunnery sergeant on the floor. "There's a cloister of nuns here in Elsinore. I'm sure they would be willing to help."

"Are you sure we can trust them?" Flem asked, not wanting to involve more people than necessary.

Katlev nodded. "The sisters have done it before."

Dr. Prestur turned toward his patient. "How do you feel about that?"

"If you think it's safe, let's do it. I'm in no position to argue."

"Where is it?" Flem asked. "How do we get there?"

"It's near Kornberg Castle," Dr. Prestur said.

Katlev pulled out a pen and began drawing a map. "A few kilometers before the castle, we'll take a road to the right."

"Kornberg Castle? Ain't that the castle Shakespeare wrote about?" the gunnery sergeant asked.

"It is," Flem said proudly. "In Hamlet."

Tyler Tamree smiled. "Then by all means, get me to the nunnery—oh, sorry, I mean to the convent."

"Great! We'll leave at daybreak," Dr. Prestur said.

"Better make that half an hour before daybreak," Katlev said. "We'll have to take the back roads and drive without our headlights."

Chapter Sixteen

At five the next morning, Katlev awoke with a stiff neck and a full bladder. His guests lay sprawled on the floor. Their heads rested on rolled up fishnets, which served also as blankets. Ignoring the arthritis in both of his knees, Katlev stepped over his sleeping guests, climbed the steps to the deck, then headed for the latrine.

When he returned, a few minutes later, he grabbed his prayer shawl off the shelf. In silence, he prayed the traditional blessing for donning a *tallit*. When he was done, he draped it over his shoulders then sat down at the table without turning on the lamp. Normally, he prayed standing, but this morning, he would pray the ancient *Amidah* silently, seated and in the dark.

Blessed are You, Adonai, our Elohim, and Elohim of our fathers, Elohim of Avraham, Elohim of Yitzchak, and Elohim of Yacov, the great, mighty, awesome, and exalted El, Who bestows bountiful kindness, Who creates all things, Who remembers the piety of the Patriarchs, and Who, in love, brings a Redeemer to their children's children, for the sake of His Name.

Sensing he was being watched, Katlev opened his eyes.

"Good morning," Flem said.

Katlev removed his *tallit*, folded it neatly, then got up. "I'll make us some coffee," he told Flem, assured that the Most High, in His mercy, would forgive him for not finishing his morning prayers. Saving a life, was a weightier matter of the Torah.

Dr. Prestur yawned, stretched, then checked his watch. As the gunnery sergeant, Tyler Tamree, continued to snore. Dr. Prestur got up and felt his patient's forehead. Katlev thought the sergeant's cheeks looked rosier than usual this morning.

Frowning, Dr. Prestur felt his patient's pulse.

"Is he okay?" Katlev asked.

The doc reached for his bag. "He's burning up. Get me some water. I'll try to get aspirin down him."

Looking worried, Flem opened the cabinet for a glass.

"I gave him a dose of penicillin last night," Dr. Prestur said, inspecting a vial. "I have enough for one more."

"We need to leave while it's still dark," Katlev said. "We'll have to carry him to your car."

Ten minutes later, as they headed north on a gravel road, the black sky became purple.

"Turn right up ahead," Katlev said. "The convent is a kilometer down that road."

Dr. Prestur gripped the wheel as he executed the curve. "Check his temperature, will you, Flem? If he is still hot, rub him down with some alcohol. You'll find a bottle of it in my bag."

Flem touched the sergeant's head. "He feels cooler to me."

"His color looks better too," Katlev noted.

"Good," Dr. Prestur said. "After I take you two back to the boat, I will go to the hospital for more supplies. The sisters will need them."

Around the next bend, a stone edifice appeared in a clearing. Katlev got out of the car and rang the convent's doorbell. A few seconds later the door opened.

"Yes? What is it?" the nun asked, glancing from Katlev to the automobile, then back at Katlev.

"We have a man with a broken leg and a fever."

"I'm sorry to hear it, but we're not a hospital."

"He is a member of the RAF."

Looking fearful, she began wringing her hands. "You must know that it's illegal to render aid to the enemy."

"Will you just look at him, Sister?" Katlev pleaded. "Dr. Prestur will provide whatever you need to nurse him. Please, Sister! Please. Tyler's in a bad way."

Her expression changed—excitement replaced fear. "Did you say Tyler?"

"Yes, Sister. Tyler Tamree. He's a RAF gunnery sergeant."

The plumpish nun flung the door wide. "Well, why didn't you say so in the first place?" she said, stepping aside. "Bring him in! We've been expecting him."

Katlev raised his eyes to heaven. "Thank you, Most Merciful!" Then he waved to the others. "Bring him in."

After tucking Tyler into a freshly made cot in an infirmary filled with the sergeant's compatriots, the nun ushered Katlev, Flem, and Dr. Prestur into the office of Mother Superior. She hurried around her desk to greet them.

"Welcome, gentlemen. Please have a seat." She motioned to some leather chairs in front of a picture window, overlooking a grotto. "You'll have to forgive Sister Lavita's reticence to let you in. We can't take any chances these days."

"Our flyers, you see," Sister Lavita explained, "usually come to us through—"

"That's enough, Sister Lavita! You may go now."

Red-faced, the young nun bowed slightly, then rushed out of Mother Superior's office.

"I'm sure you can appreciate our need for secrecy," Mother Superior explained as she sat down behind her desk.

"Rest assured," Dr. Prestur said, "we won't give you away."

"You won't intentionally, I'm sure. But the Gestapo's interrogation methods fall notoriously short of the Geneva Convention's guidelines. So, we operate on a need-to-know basis."

"We understand," Katlev said. "We're here to offer our assistance, to join the Underground. My fishing boat will be at your disposal."

"I'm a doctor," Juhl explained. "Feel free to call on me at any time, day or night."

Mother Superior beamed. "The Lord can always use an extra pair of hands. Leave me your names and addresses. We will contact you as soon as you've all been vetted."

"Do you need medical supplies?" Dr. Prestur asked.

"Right now we're in good shape. But that could change at any time. I'll let you know if we start to run low."

"I gave him a shot of penicillin less than an hour ago," Dr. Prestur said. "And he had one last night."

"Never fear, the young man's needs will be met. We have a physician who stops by twice a day when we have, shall we say, 'guests to entertain?' "

~*~*~

An hour after they left the convent in Elsinore, Katlev set his course for Copenhagen. The sky was clear, and the waters calm. Never before had Flem felt so alive, so exhilarated. Katlev sensed it too. Flem could tell by his posture as he stood tall at the helm.

"You're feeling what I'm feeling, aren't you?"

"I've lived with regret for half a century, wondering what might have happened had I not been a coward."

"You're no coward," Flem said. "I've seen you in action. There's no one more faithful than you."

"I knew what the Most High wanted me to do. I didn't do it, Flem, and Sima died."

"You've been forgiven."

"Yes, but I've not forgotten. Not a day goes by I don't think about Jacob. He might have been saved, might have married Sima, if I'd been obedient, and now he's rotting in a concentration camp."

"You don't know that, Katlev. You said so yourself he may have left Germany."

"His life has been ruined. Jacob is a bitter man because of me."

"Then why do you look so excited?"

Katlev beamed. "Because the Most High, blessed be He, is giving me another chance. I feel it in my bones, Flem! He has something huge for me to do, for us to do," he said, glancing at Flem.

"And this time, I won't run away from it!" Excitement danced in his eyes. "Whatever Elohim wants, wherever He needs me to go, I will put all that I am and all that I have at His disposal."

"And you will, Katlev! We will! To quote Mordechai, who knows that we haven't been called to the kingdom for such a time as this."

The old man's eyes filled with tears. "I could hug you for that, my boy," Katlev said as the current shifted the boat leeward, "but I can't let go of this wheel."

~*~*~

Worried because Flem and her father were supposed to have been back early that morning, Liesel put on her jacket. It was already four in the afternoon and no one had heard from either of them. Liesel's mother was a basket case, and now Liesel had to break the news to Flem's parents. They had a right to know.

She felt around in her pocket. Finding her handkerchief, she pulled it out and gave her nose a good blow. Her legs felt as if they weighed a ton as she walked through her back gate to the Lunds' house.

"Is something wrong?" Mrs. Lund asked when she opened her kitchen door to find Liesel standing there. "Has something happened? Is it Flem?"

"May I sit down?" Liesel asked, her knees feeling weak.

Mrs. Lund pulled out a chair at the table. "May I pour you some tea?"

"I'll have water, if you don't mind."

"Certainly." Mrs. Lund brought it to her, then took a seat across from her guest.

Liesel took a sip then set her glass down, knowing she couldn't put this off any longer. "Flem and Katlev smuggled Sven Lillelund into Sweden last night. My father helped them. They were due back this morning, but no one has heard from them."

Tears welled in Mrs. Lund's eyes. "I can't lose my son."

Liesel dropped to her knees and put her arms around the woman. "We have to pray. That's all we can do."

"You pray! I can't even speak," Flem's mother sobbed.

"Dear Lord Jesus, I know You are with us, in our midst. It says so in Your Word. We're gathered in Your Name. We beg You to please send Flem, my father, and Katlev home. Nothing is impossible for You. Your mercies are new every morning, the Bible says."

"If You are the Messiah, please send my son back to me, and I will worship You, too. Just send him home."

Liesel's spirit soared as her grief turned to joy. Surely, the Lord would answer such a heartfelt prayer. "Amen and amen," Liesel said. She opened her eyes and threw her arms around her future mother-in-law. Then a shadow fell across the kitchen floor.

Flem's father stood in the doorway. The expression in his eyes was one Liesel had seen before, on the face of a lone survivor of a car crash.

"Flem is missing," Mrs. Lund explained tearfully. "I didn't know what else to do, Sol."

Mr. Lund remained silent, as if in a daze.

"Your son and Katlev smuggled a member of the Resistance into Sweden last night. They were supposed to get back this morning, but we haven't heard from them yet."

Mr. Lund turned and left the room.

"I'd better go to him," Mrs. Lund said, using her apron to wipe her tears.

Liesel felt terrible. Now Flem's father would hate her even more. Fresh tears blurred Liesel's vision as the Lunds' kitchen door opened. Liesel turned to see who it was.

Chapter Seventeen

George Duckwitz pushed his chair back from his dining room table. From the moment he learned about the impending roundup of the Jews, food had lost its flavor and sleep its repose.

"Where are you going?" his wife asked. "You hardly touched your supper."

"I'm not hungry."

"But you were the one who insisted we eat early."

"A man can change his mind."

"You're driving me crazy, George! This nonsense has to stop!"

Ignoring his wife, George went out onto the balcony to watch the boats bob in the harbor. The sun hung low on the horizon. It would be dark soon, he thought as he leaned against the rail. He knew he must act. But do what? Warn the Jews? Where would they go?

Sweden was neutral, in theory at least. Still, they armed the Finns to fight the Russians when Hitler requested it then denied petrol to Norway. How neutral was that? He'd heard from a reliable source, just last week, that the Swedish minister in Buenos Aires was sending coded messages for the Reich, directing German U-boat attacks on allied shipping.

George lit a cigarette. Maybe he should fly to Stockholm and beg his friend, Ekblad, to arrange a private meeting with Sweden's prime minister. Perhaps, he could convince him to accept Denmark's Jews.

~*~*~

Flem was exhausted when he entered his parents' kitchen, but the joy on his mother's face revived him. "What's going on?" he asked.

"You're alive!" Liesel exclaimed. "We've been so worried," she said, throwing her arms around him.

"I'm so sorry. I never meant for you to worry. Either of you," he added, beckoning his mother to join in their hug. As soon as she did, Inger barged into the kitchen.

"Is it true?" she demanded.

"Is what true?" Flem asked.

"Not you!" Inger looked like she wanted to strangle him. "I'm talking to Aunt Nettie."

"Inger, what is it, dear?" his mother asked, turning to face the enraged teenager.

"Is what Uncle Sol just told me true?"

"What did he say?"

"That you were praying to Jesus."

His mother glanced from Inger to Liesel, then turned to Flem. "I thought you were dead."

"Did you pray to Jesus?" Inger demanded.

"Did you, Mother?" Flem asked elated.

"I prayed to Jesus," Liesel explained.

"Then it's not true?" Inger challenged.

His mother sighed. "It's okay, Liesel, I must tell the truth. After Liesel prayed, I said that if He was the Messiah and would send you home that I would believe in Him too."

"No! You can't do this," Inger cried, stomping her foot. "You can't!"

His mother grabbed the girl's wrist and shook it. "Would you rather my prayer not have been answered?"

Angrily, Inger extricated herself and ran out of the kitchen.

Flem stood there dazed, delighted about his mother and worried about his father.

118

"I'd better go to my husband," his mother said, "and try to make him understand. I don't know how much more the poor man can take after what happened earlier."

"What do you mean? What happened?" Flem asked.

"The S.S. shut down our Community Center and took the list of our addresses. Your father was there. He saw it happen."

Flem and Liesel exchanged looks.

"I'll talk to Aldur," Liesel said.

"I thought he moved out," Flem replied.

"He moved in with his girlfriend's parents, but if anyone knows what these Germans are up to, he will."

Flem frowned, skeptically. "And you expect him to tell you?"

"I can wheedle it out of him. Trust me."

"Where can we hide that the Germans won't find us?" his mother asked, tearfully.

"Sweden," Flem said. "If Liesel can find out when they plan to make their move, we can leave the day before."

"What if there isn't time? What if they're coming for us tonight?" his mother asked.

"Relax, Mother. Have faith."

"I'll go to the University in the morning and speak to my brother before he leaves for work."

"What about your job at the hospital?" Flem asked.

Liesel shrugged. "I'll have father explain that something came up."

"I'll ask Katlev to stay docked until we hear from you, just in case we have to move quickly."

"This is happening so fast," his mother said. "How can I leave my home? Everything I love is here."

Flem grabbed her shoulders. "Listen to yourself, Mother. One minute you're complaining there's no solution and when we offer one, you're lamenting over what? Leaving your china?"

"You think this is easy, Flem? We've worked all our lives to get what we have, so forgive me if I'm not overjoyed at the thought of leaving it all behind."

"I don't like it any better than you do, Mother, but what choice do we have? We can either leave or end up in a concentration camp."

"Pastor Uri says we're not to ask why when terrible things happen. We're to ask what. What should I learn? What should I do?"

"I am sure your pastor is right," his mother said, placing one hand on each of their cheeks. "Don't worry about me. I'll be fine. I just need a little time to cry…and to pray."

~*~*~

The next morning, Liesel parked her bicycle in one of the racks outside the main entrance to the university. She glanced at her watch. Aldur should be getting out of his last class at any moment. She went in to wait for him, praying her plan would work. It had to! Her future—and that of her soon-to-be husband and in-laws—depended on it. A few minutes later, when Aldur exited his class, Liesel rushed over to him.

"What are you doing here? I thought you dropped out of school," he said, sneering.

"We need to talk," Liesel said as her brother studied her skeptically. "Can't you see how badly I feel? I want to make amends?"

When his smirk finally relaxed, Liesel knew he would capitulate. Then an all-too-familiar voice called his name.

Liesel glanced over her shoulder and saw Ursula sashaying through the crowd in a clingy red sweater. Her peekaboo Veronica Lake hairdo hung over her face like a parted curtain.

"What a surprise," Ursula said. "I heard you got a job at the hospital."

"I'm here to see my brother."

"Well, make it quick. We're meeting some friends at Tivoli amusement park."

Liesel turned to her brother. "I thought you were working today."

"My schedule changed."

"I must talk to you in private, please, Aldur!" She placed a hand on her brother's arm. "I won't keep you long. I promise."

Aldur glanced at his watch, and Liesel knew he would agree.

He turned to Ursula. "I'll meet you in front of the Ferris wheel at eleven-thirty,"

"Make it one-thirty," she replied looking peeved. "There's someone I must talk to as well." With a toss of her head, she stalked off.

So far, so good, Liesel thought. She breathed a sigh of relief. Now, comes the hard part.

~*~*~

As they rode their bikes to a nearby café, Liesel tried to decide if she should stick to her original strategy or lay all of her cards on the table. It was only a hunch, but her brother's attitude seemed somewhat mellowed.

As soon as they sat down, the waitress took their order. As she walked away, Liesel leaned forward and placed her hand on her brother's arm. "Mother told me about that letter you found."

Aldur stiffened.

"Father confirmed it," Liesel continued.

"How is Mother?"

"She misses you."

"I've been meaning to stop by," he said, lowering his gaze.

"She's forgiven him, Aldur. Why won't you?"

He pulled his arm away, glaring at her. "A woman and her child are dead!"

"The woman committed suicide."

"Because of him!" he said, raising his voice.

"She pulled her scheme before, Aldur. Mr. Andersen, the administrator at the hospital can verify it."

"What does he have to do with this?"

"Our father wasn't the first married doctor this woman had an affair with. She told the other one she was pregnant, too."

"How does Mr. Anderson figure into this?"

"After Father refused to marry her, she went to see Mr. Anderson, hoping he would pressure Father to do the right thing, and he did. Only not what she wanted. Mr. Anderson threatened to have her arrested for extortion!"

"Extortion?"

"The first doctor paid the woman off, so she could go away and have the child."

"She already had a child?"

"After she cashed the check, she told him she miscarried."

Aldur stared back at his sister in silence.

"Don't you see, Aldur? It was all a scam."

Her brother began combing his fingers through his hair. "Father tried to explain this to me, but I thought he was lying."

"Father knows he was wrong. Remember how miserable he was after Mother left?" Liesel asked as the waitress returned with their drinks.

Aldur sipped his lager in silence.

"He loves you, Aldur, and so do I."

Her brother took another sip.

"You should come home."

"Father threw me out."

"He'll take you back if you'll talk to him. I want you home, too, just be civil to Flem."

Aldur's jaw twitched. "Is that what this is all about?"

"You used to be friends."

"He is a Jew!" Aldur said, raising his voice again. Several patrons turned to stare at them.

"So is Jesus!" she retorted, not caring who was listening.

Aldur pushed back his chair. He stood and threw some money on the table.

"I'm marrying him, Aldur. Whether you like it or not, you will be an uncle to our children."

"You'll never get the chance," he said and stormed out of the café.

Determined to find out what he meant by never get the chance, Liesel followed her brother outside. As he mounted his bicycle, she cried, "Please, Aldur, I must talk to you."

"Talk to your boyfriend," he yelled back as he rode away.

She hopped on her bike and pedaled as fast as she could. She had to catch up with him, had to find out if he knew what the Germans were planning, and more importantly when they planned to do it. Finally, Aldur stopped for a red light halfway down the block, and she caught up to him.

"Why won't you talk to me?" she asked breathlessly.

"You think I don't know when I'm being used?"

"But I do miss you."

"What a liar you are!"

"I miss the brother you used to be."

When the light turned green, Aldur began pedaling faster than before. Clearing the intersection, he turned and yelled something over his shoulder. Only Liesel never heard it. All she heard was a blast from the front driver's-side tire of the automobile next to her. As it swerved into her lane, she fell, losing consciousness.

Chapter Eighteen

The words he had just shouted ripped Aldur's heart out. He hopped off his bike and pushed it back across the intersection to the sidewalk where several men had carried his sister's body. After pushing through the gathering crowd, he knelt next to her. His tears fell onto his sister's face, mixing with a small trickle of blood coming from the right corner of her mouth.

"You know this woman?" a German officer demanded standing over him. Aldur recognized him immediately. He was one of the soldiers in the car with the blowout.

"She's my sister," Aldur told him.

"I'll call for an ambulance," a woman said, then turned and ran into the barbershop behind them.

His sister's eyelids fluttered but did not open. Then another German staff car pulled up to the curb. As two more German officers hopped out, the woman making the call returned. "An ambulance will be here in ten minutes."

"I found these in the street. She must have had them in her basket," an elderly gentleman said, placing some books on the sidewalk next to her.

Liesel moaned.

"Can you hear me?" Aldur asked, searching her face. Her lips moved slightly, as if she was trying to form words. Only no sound came out. "I didn't mean it, Liesel. I swear I didn't. Please forgive me," he begged as a German soldier knelt beside him.

"The hospital's not far. We could take you both there if you don't want to wait for that ambulance."

"That would be great," Aldur said, appreciatively.

"It's the least we can do under the circumstances," the soldier replied as he picked up one of the books next to her. " *'Cooking for Rosh Hashanah.'* You are Jews!"

"No!" Aldur said. "We are Lutherans!"

"Then how do you explain this?" he asked, shoving the book at Aldur.

"I can't! But we are not Jews! You must believe me."

The soldier stood and dusted off his trousers. "Let's go," he told the others. "We have wasted enough time here."

"What about my sister?"

"She had better watch where she is going next time," he said. Then he gave the salute: "Heil Hitler!"

~*~*~

"Dr. Prestur, report to emergency. Dr. Prestur to emergency."

Now what? Juhl thought. He wasn't scheduled to work in the E.R. until next week. He slipped the boy's chart back into the holder at the foot of his bed.

"Am I going to live, Doc?"

Juhl smiled. "I think so, Martin," he told the precocious eight-year old with the cast on his leg. "But no more jumping out of trees."

"The limb broke. I didn't jump."

Juhl ruffled the boy's hair. "Then, no more climbing trees."

Several minutes later, Juhl pushed open the stark-white double doors that led to the emergency waiting area.

"Dr. Prestur, I am afraid there has been an accident," a resident said, rushing over to him.

"This is an emergency room, isn't it?" he quipped, then noticed Aldur pacing outside an examination room down the corridor.

"It's your daughter," the intern explained. "She swerved trying to get out of the way of a car and was knocked off her bicycle. I'm afraid she is still unconscious."

"My son was with her?"

The intern nodded. "He's pretty shaken. I suggested he take a sedative, but he refused."

"Thanks," Juhl said. "I'll take it from here." On what felt like rubber legs, he hurried to his son's side and opened his arms. Aldur dove into them.

"I didn't mean what I told her, Father. I swear I didn't mean it."

"God can forgive you, Son, whatever you said. You have only to ask."

"But you don't know what I said."

"God knows. Now let's go see your sister."

"They won't let me in."

"They will now. You're with me," Juhl assured him as an orderly ran past them.

"The ban on phone calls has been lifted," he shouted excitedly, as he ran down the hall. "It was just announced on the radio."

At least one good thing had happened, Juhl thought, opening the door to his daughter's room.

Chapter Nineteen

"As far as we can tell," Dr. Colbertsen told them, "she has no internal injuries."

"But she was bleeding from her mouth," Aldur said.

"She might have bitten her tongue. Her vital signs are stable. Her blood count and chemistry profile are normal, even her x-rays. If there's hemorrhaging or swelling in the brain, it's minuscule."

"Then why is she still unconscious?" Juhl asked.

Dr. Colbertsen shrugged, then placed a hand on Juhl's back. "We'll take more x-rays in a couple of hours. I'll let you know if there are any changes."

Juhl stared at his motionless daughter. "Well, I better call my wife since the ban has been lifted."

"I can call Deidre for you," Dr. Colbertsen offered.

"Thanks, but I better do this myself."

"Wait, Father!" Aldur checked his wristwatch. "I can take a cab and be home in fifteen minutes, that way she won't be alone when you call."

"Good idea," Juhl said, proud of his son as he headed for the door. "And bring her back. By then, we might have better news."

"I will," Aldur promised.

Juhl bent over and kissed his daughter's forehead, then realized that he had better try to reach Flem.

~*~*~

Back on the cutter, Flem's stomach was in knots as he stared at the calm sea. "I don't understand why she's not here yet," he told Katlev. "Something must have gone wrong. I'm going to her house."

"Do you want me to go with you?"

"No. Stay here in case she shows up. I'll be back as soon as I can."

Katlev grabbed his arm. "Don't you think we should pray first?"

~*~*~

Flem had never pedaled so fast—and hoped he never would again. His throat burned as well as his thighs, but the pain would be worth it if Liesel's mother could lay his worries to rest. Not wanting to greet her all sweaty, he wiped his face then stuffed the handkerchief in his pocket and rapped on the door.

No one answered. He knocked harder. Still no response. Thinking he should leave a note, he checked his pockets for something to write on. Finding nothing, he sat down on the steps to wait.

"Flem?" his mother called to him from the living room window. "If you're waiting for Mrs. Prestur, she left a little while ago in a taxi."

"Was Liesel with her?"

"No. Aldur was. What's going on? She looked upset."

"Do you know where they went?"

"No, but there was blood on Aldur's jacket."

"Blood?" Flem's heart began to hammer.

"That's what it looked like."

Flem sprang to his feet.

"Where are you going?" his mother asked as he mounted his bicycle.

"To the hospital. Liesel was supposed to speak to Aldur this morning and meet me at the boat afterwards. But she never showed up."

"Why don't you call first? The ban has been lifted."

"It has?" Flem said, stunned by the unexpected good news. "I'll be right there." He dismounted his bike. A few seconds later, Inger opened the door. The teenager was unsmiling but not hostile. His mother held out the receiver. Flem grabbed it then dialed the operator. After a long minute, Dr. Prestur came on the wire.

"Have you heard from Liesel?" Flem asked. "She was supposed to meet us at the boat but never showed up."

When Dr. Prestur didn't answer right away, Flem gripped the receiver tighter.

"I was about to call you, Flem. I'm afraid there has been an accident. Liesel is in a coma."

"In a coma?"

Mrs. Lund gasped.

"I'll be right there," Flem told him and hung up.

"Call a taxi, Inger," his mother said. "We're going with you," she told her son.

"Is Liesel going to die?" Inger asked, after calling for their taxi. Flem raised his hand to strike her. Then he noticed her tears and dropped his arm. "No. Now, hurry up and get ready to leave."

~*~*~

Deidre leaned over the bedrails watching her daughter breathe. How could this have happened? "She has to wake up," she told Juhl, "she just has to."

He placed his hand on her shoulder and gave it a squeeze. "I'm going to call Pastor Uri and let him know what's happened. Will you be okay?"

Deidre nodded. "Just don't be long."

"I won't," he promised. "But the more people we have praying the better I will feel."

"Why?" Aldur asked. "Does God heal based on numbers?"

Wanting to choke him, Deidre shot him a deadly look.

"This is no time for sarcasm, Aldur!" Juhl warned.

"Who's being sarcastic? I really don't understand why people always say that."

"Then ask your mother," Juhl said and left the room.

"I wish you would be civil," Deidre said sternly. "For your sister's sake, if nothing else."

Aldur shrugged. "How was I not civil? All I did was ask a question."

"It's your attitude! It's gone on long enough. Let go of the past, Aldur!"

"I have, Mother."

Deidre opened her eyes wide. "You have? When did this miracle happen?"

"Today, after Liesel's accident."

Deidre's anger evaporated. She flung her arms around her son and hugged him. Then almost as quickly she pulled back and looked him in the eye. "Does your father know about this?"

Aldur shrugged. "I don't know…he might suspect it."

"You haven't told him?"

"Not yet."

"Is the accident what brought you to your senses?"

"I suppose. That and what Liesel told me earlier."

"What did she say?

"She told me about the other doctor that woman had an affair with."

"Oh, I see," Deidre said, releasing her son.

"And she told me about Flem."

Deidre tensed. "What about Flem?"

Aldur walked over to his sister's bed and stared down at her motionless body. "That she plans to marry him and that you and Father have given her your consent."

Deidre placed a hand on her son's shoulder. "Flem will make her a good husband, Aldur."

"But he's a Jew!"

"Don't start that again. I won't have it, Aldur. Do you hear?"

"I know, and I'm sorry. I didn't mean it the way it sounded. It's just that we are Lutherans."

"We are Christians, Aldur. And so is Flem."

130

Aldur stared at her incredulously. "Flem, a Christian? How is that possible? He's a Jew."

"Yes and no—it's complicated. I'm sure your sister would rather explain it herself."

"Did he convert?"

"Not exactly. Like I said, it's complicated." How could she explain this?

"Either he has or he hasn't, Mother!"

"Not according to your sister," Deidre said, praying for the right words. "Let's sit down." She led him to some chairs by the window. "I'll try to explain it.

~*~*~

"He's making it up, Mother! Can't you see that?"

"Making what up?" his mother said.

"It's a ruse to get Liesel back. I can't believe you fell for it."

"Fell for what?"

"All this nonsense about believing in Jesus and still being a Jew!" Aldur said. "He wants his cake and to eat it too."

Sparks flashed in his mother's eyes. "Get out. I mean it. Now, before I box your ears."

"I have to stay with Liesel. I must be here when she wakes up."

"I don't want you anywhere near her. Do you hear me? Not until you change. Not until you become the boy I raised."

His mother poked him in his chest, then began to cry. He wanted to comfort her but knew better.

"You might have forgiven your father, and that's wonderful, but it's not enough. Not for me! I want my son back! My Aldur! You're not him! My Aldur had a soul, a beautiful soul."

His mother's words crushed him. He wanted to cry but couldn't. He felt dry, empty, hollow inside. Was she right? Had he lost his soul? Aldur opened the door to leave and found Flem on the other side, looking bewildered.

"Come in, Flem," his mother said. "Aldur was just leaving."

Chapter Twenty

Flem rushed to Liesel's bedside. Her expression was serene, but her face was badly bruised. He wanted to hold her but couldn't bear the thought of causing her more pain. So, he stroked her hair. "How did it happen?"

"She fell off her bike trying to get out of the way of a car that blew a tire. Aldur saw the whole thing." Mrs. Prestur sighed. "Her vital signs are stable. She has no internal bleeding, not even a broken bone. She just can't wake up."

"It's my fault. I never should've agreed."

"Agreed to what?" Mrs. Prestur asked as Dr. Prestur came into the room.

"I just saw your mother and cousin in the waiting room," he told Flem. "Why don't you have them come in?"

"The nurse won't allow it," Flem explained. "Too many people at one time."

"Then, we'll go. I need to speak to my wife in private, anyway. Come, Deidre." Dr. Prestur took her arm. "Let's get some coffee. There is something I need to tell you."

"We'll finish our conversation later," Mrs. Prestur told Flem.

"Of course," he assured her, figuring he could bring in his mother and Inger to stay with Liesel while he made a phone call.

~*~*~

Knowing he didn't have much time, and hoping his wife would understand, Juhl took Deidre's hand. "Let's go to my office."

"I thought we were getting coffee."

"I have to tell you something, and I don't want it overheard."

Deidre stopped in her tracks. "Is it about Liesel?"

"No, darling, just something we need to keep under wraps, and I don't have much time."

Several minutes later, when they entered Juhl's suite, the waiting area was empty except for the cleaning lady swabbing the floor.

"Excuse me, do you know where my nurse went?" Juhl asked.

"To autoclave is what she said," the woman replied, continuing her work.

He checked his watch. "How long ago did she leave?"

"Five, maybe ten minutes ago."

That didn't leave him much time. "Thanks," he said, leading Deidre into his office.

"What is going on? You're frightening me, Juhl, with all this intrigue."

Juhl locked the door, then removed his stethoscope and laid it on his desk. "I got a message from the nun I told you about," he said, removing his lab coat. "The Underground has a job for me to do. I have to leave right away."

"But our daughter is unconscious."

"If I don't go now, two men might die. Do you want that on your conscience?"

"I want my little girl whole."

Juhl pulled her into his arms. "I do too, Deidre. But we're already doing everything that can be done for her, and I don't need to be here to pray."

"What about me? I need you, too!"

Somehow, he had to make her understand how important his mission was without telling her about the doctor who had been killed. If she knew, she would never let him leave. "I can't tell you anything more. It would put too many people at risk. Please, Deidre, you have to trust me on this. I'll be back as soon as I can. I promise."

"What do I tell people when they ask me where you are?"

"Tell them I've gone to Elsinore." It was as much of the truth as he could share. "Say I'm consulting a colleague about Liesel."

"What about Flem and Katlev? Aren't they part of your group?"

"They only need a doctor for this mission."

Tears spilled from Deidre's eyes. "Be careful," she whispered and threw herself into his arms.

"You'll have Aldur with you until I get back," he said, holding her tightly.

"No, I won't. I threw him out. I had to put my foot down."

That wasn't what Juhl wanted to hear. He'd been so certain that Aldur had had a change of heart.

"Well, go on." She pushed him away. "Or do you want me to start crying again?"

"I hate leaving you, but there are lives at stake."

"I know, Juhl. I know."

"We're in a war and we have to win."

"Go! I'll be okay."

Hating the war now more than ever, he kissed her goodbye then unlocked the door.

~*~*~

"Ahoy, anyone aboard?"

"I'm in the cabin," Katlev replied, not recognizing the voice. He shut his Bible as a boy of about sixteen sprinted down the steps.

"You Katlev Hertz?"

"I was the last time I checked. Who wants to know?"

"I'm a busboy at Helweg's Café. I got a message for you. Some fellow named Fleming Lund needs you at Bispebjerg Hospital."

"Bispebjerg Hospital? Is he hurt?"

"Some girl is. He wants you to leave right away. He also said you would give me a kroner for delivering the message."

Katlev fished in his pocket. "Here, take two," he said, handing him the coins. "Call me a cab when you get back to the café."

"I already have. It should be here any minute."

~*~*~

In a closet in his father's office, Aldur waited, barely breathing. He listened to make sure his parents had left. Why hadn't he made his presence known? What was he going to do now? His father was working with the Resistance, a crime punishable by death!

Certain that they were gone, Aldur opened the closet to find the old charwoman staring at him accusingly. "Why were you hiding in that closet? You told me you were waiting for your father."

Humiliated, Aldur knew he would have to buy the old crone's silence. He dug into his pocket. Outside, in the corridor, he pulled out the apology he'd written to his parents just before they came in. With disgust, he tore the letter in half, glanced both ways to make sure no one was watching him, then tossed it into a trashcan.

As Aldur walked away, he thought better of it. He returned and pulled it out of the trash. This time, he ripped it into smaller pieces, then separately dropped each piece into the basket. Satisfied that no one would piece it together now, he aimlessly began pacing again.

Where could he go? He never felt so alone. And he couldn't leave the hospital without seeing his sister. Then he remembered the chapel. It was the only place in the hospital he could rest while he tried to figure out what he should do.

~*~*~

When the door opened, Flem glanced over his shoulder, fearing it was Aldur returning. He relaxed when he saw Katlev. The old man removed a small flask from his jacket, unscrewed the cap then dabbed a sweet-scented oil on Liesel's forehead.

"Heal us, Adonai, and we will be healed," Katlev prayed with his hand still on her head. "Save us and we will be saved, for You are our praise. Grant perfect healing against all our ailments, for You, Almighty King, are a faithful and merciful healer. Blessed are You, Elohim, the healer of the sick of Your people, Israel."

Flem turned away, fighting back tears.

"It's okay," Katlev told him, placing his hand on Flem's

shoulder. "Yeshua wept, didn't He? And don't forget Sima. She, too, was unconscious when Yeshua healed her."

"You're right. I should've been praying over her all this time," Flem said as the door opened again. He relaxed when he saw it was only the doctor and two nurses.

"I have to examine my patient. Will you please step out of the room?"

"Of course," Flem said. "We'll be right outside if you need us."

"Actually, there is something you can do for me. I just sent Mrs. Prestur to the cafeteria. Would you check on her, Flem? Encourage her to eat something. She looks exhausted."

"I will," Flem promised.

"We may as well eat something too," Katlev said.

"You go ahead," Flem told him. "Order me whatever you're having, and I will join you in a few minutes. I just need to pray first. Do you know how to get there?"

"I'll find it," Katlev assured him.

On his way to the chapel, Flem spotted his mother and cousin sitting in the waiting room.

"How is she, Flem?" his mother asked as he approached them. She reached for his hand and he grasped it.

"No change yet, but she'll come out of it soon. I know she will."

"It's all my fault," Inger said.

"Shush!" his mother said. "You must stop saying such things."

"What do you mean?" Flem asked the girl, but his cousin would not look at him. "Why did you say that, Inger?"

"It's only guilt talking," his mother said, "nothing more."

"Guilt about what?" Flem demanded in a hushed tone, aware that others were listening. "What have you done, Inger?"

Slowly, the teenager raised her head. "Promise you won't hate me?"

"Just tell me what you've done!"

"I wished Liesel dead. Only I didn't mean it, Flem. I swear I didn't! Please, you must believe me," she begged.

His cousin's tears diluted his anger. "You didn't cause her

accident, Inger, and Liesel is not going to die," he declared calmly, then turned to his mother. "Why don't you two go to the cafeteria? Katlev is there now, ordering for me. I'll join you shortly. I have something to do first."

"Katlev is here?" Inger looked anxious again. "Here in the hospital?"

"He is, and you better treat him with respect. Do you hear me?"

Inger's cheeks turned red. She nodded and lowered her head.

His mother glanced at her watch. "I should telephone your father and let him know we won't be home for dinner. He can warm up some leftovers."

"Why don't you invite him to join us? He'll refuse, of course, but at least he will know that he isn't being excluded. I have to go now. I'll join you in a few minutes."

"Wait!" his mother said. "How will we know this Katlev fellow?"

"Look for an old man with a weathered face and a gray beard. You can't miss him."

Chapter Twenty-one

Aldur heard the door to the chapel open and shut as he lay on the back pew. He opened his eyes to find Fleming Lund gazing toward the altar. Debating whether he should make his presence known, he watched in silence. When Lund moved out of his field of vision, Aldur stealthily sat up.

Outside, the clouds that had been blocking the sun all day, moved out of the way. Light streamed through the chapel's stained-glass windows, blinding Aldur for a moment. He had to get out of there, now, while Lund's back was still toward him. He positioned himself to make his getaway, then froze when he heard what sounded like weeping.

~*~*~

Uncontrollable grief washed over Flem. His heart broke for all the evil in the world. Was this a taste of the agony Yeshua endured on the cross? "Father, forgive them," he prayed. "They know not what they do because they don't know You. If they did, they wouldn't hate."

With these few spoken words, Flem's burden lifted. At peace but drained, he laid his head down on the altar rail. Behind him, he heard the chapel door open then close.

~*~*~

Aldur remembered that an adjoining corridor up ahead led to the parking lot. Once outside, he hoped he'd be able to breathe again. The parking lot was nearly empty. He leaned forward and pressed his palms against his thighs. But his breathing became more jagged as the accusing words came faster and louder, echoing through his mind. *You have Aldur with you until I get back. No, I won't! I threw him out. Aldur has no soul!*

Aldur covered his ears. But the voices did not stop. *Aldur has no soul! Your sister's going to die. Aldur has no soul! Your sister will die. You murdered her with your words! Aldur has no soul. I threw him out. Father, forgive them, they don't know what they do. They hate because they don't know You!*

"Stop it! Stop!" Aldur shouted. "I didn't mean what I said. I'm sorry! Okay? I'm so sorry." Tears ran down his cheeks. "Please let my sister live," he begged. "I want my soul back."

Sweet silence ensued, as if Aldur had just awakened from a nightmare. Then a still, small voice, one rich in mercy, whispered, "Your exile has ended. It's time to go home."

~*~*~

Flem looked around the cafeteria and spotted Katlev waving to him from a table against the wall. As he approached, conversation stopped.

"Did something happen?" his mother asked. She looked at him quizzically. "Your eyes are puffy."

"Well, it was the strangest thing," Flem replied, pulling out a chair to join them. "I went to the chapel to pray for Liesel, but as soon as I knelt at the altar an unspeakable sorrow gripped me. I felt like Yeshua was praying through me."

Inger nervously moved food around on her plate.

"Isn't that crazy?" Flem asked.

Katlev set down his glass. "It's not crazy."

Inger stopped playing with her peas. "What were you sorry for?"

"Sorry for?" Flem repeated.

"You said you felt unspeakable sorrow. Sorrow for what?"

"All the evil in the world. I felt like I was repenting for every sin ever committed."

"Why? You're not responsible. Not for every sin," Inger said.

"Elohim burdened your cousin with a spirit of intercession," Katlev explained. "He was blessed to be used in this way, Inger. The Most High, blessed be He, used Flem for His purpose."

"What purpose?" Inger asked skeptically.

"I don't know," Katlev said. "But rest assured, the Lord will reveal it in His time."

~*~*~

After their meal, Flem went in to say goodnight to Liesel while the others waited in the lobby. Even with all of her bruises, Liesel was a beauty.

"Come back to me, Liesel, and I'll go with you anywhere, even to Sweden if that is what you really want."

Liesel's eyelids fluttered.

Flem held his breath, but there was no further motion.

"We've turned a corner with Inger," he said softly. "She asked for forgiveness for the way she's been acting. She wants you to get better and was even civil to Katlev tonight."

Then the door opened, and Aldur came in.

"Her eyelids just fluttered. Twice," Flem told him.

"They did?" Aldur walked over to the other side of the bed. "Can you hear me, Liesel? I have so much to tell you." He looked at Flem. "Do you mind if I have a little time alone with my sister?"

"Sure," Flem said, delighted with Aldur's new civility. "I have to speak to your father before I leave anyway."

"He's not here. He left over an hour ago."

"Are you certain?"

"He had something important to do," Aldur said. Then his hands began to tremble on the bedrail, causing it to rattle.

"Are you all right?" Flem asked.

140

Aldur let go, turned and headed for the door, just as his mother came in. Without a word, he rushed past her.

Mrs. Prestur looked confused. "Was he in here causing trouble again?"

"No! He was cordial, then all of a sudden, he started shaking."

"Shaking?"

Flem shrugged.

"You better tell me exactly what happened, Flem. Start at the beginning."

"Well, he asked if he could speak to Liesel, alone. I told him he could, and that I needed to speak to his father. Then he said Dr. Prestur wasn't here, that he left about an hour ago."

"How did he know that?"

Flem shrugged again. "He said Dr. Prestur had something important to do. After that, his hands started shaking. When I asked if he was okay, he ran out of the room. That's when you came in."

Deflating like a balloon, Mrs. Prestur made her way to a chair and collapsed into it. "He must know," she said, staring into space. "Only how?"

"Know what?" Flem asked.

Tears filled her eyes.

"I can't tell you, Flem. My husband has sworn me to secrecy."

Chapter Twenty-two

Czechoslovakia
Theresienstadt Concentration Camp

On an unusually clear night, Major Ratzinger stood outside the Sudeten barracks and puffed on his cigarette, staring at the mountain range that bordered the Czech Republic and Germany, longing for tomorrow night, when he would board a train for Berlin and leave this godforsaken place behind. A man could take only so much, and the major had reached his limit. But tonight, he must deal with one more shipment of Jews. He got up and ground out his cigarette, then returned to the barracks.

Constructed originally as a military garrison of the Austrian Empire in 1780, Theresienstadt was surrounded by two brick walls separated by a moat. In October 1941, Berlin turned Terezin into a ghetto for selected Jews in the protectorates of Bohemia, Moravia, and the greater German Reich. In February of 1942, Hitler converted the ghetto into a prison camp—his "model" prison camp. There Hitler housed elite Jews, Jews the Kaiser and the Weimar Republic had commended. Many were recipients of the Iron Cross for heroism during WWI. Others were brilliant scientists, famous writers, renowned artists, and prominent musicians. It was also a clearinghouse for elderly Jews, who would be transported to death camps in Auschwitz, Buchenwald, and Dachau.

Giving the obligatory salute, Major Ratzinger addressed the newest member of the Altestenrat, a self-governing body of Jews that Prague appointed to carry out the ghetto's administration.

"Where is Edelstein?" Ratzinger asked.

"I'm afraid a situation came up. But he should be back any minute. Is there something I can do for you in the meantime?"

"We have a shipment coming in the morning—800 of them. We'll house them for two days then transfer them to Buchenwald."

"I'll be sure to let Edelstein know."

"The Jews in Jager and Magdeberg barracks have to be moved in here and Podmokly by the end of the month to make room for the Jews coming from Denmark."

"But we're overcrowded as it is."

"Don't you think I know that?" Ratzinger yelled. What could he do? He was under orders, like everyone else. "Now just do it!"

He gave the salute and hurried out of the barracks, trying to escape memories of emaciated bodies. Barracks with no heat. No water. Eighty men crammed into one rat-infested room. Worst of all was the stench of burning flesh.

~*~*~

Early the next morning at Bohusovice Train Station, outside of Theresienstadt, a train screeched, metal grinding metal, to a full stop. As the doors opened, sunlight flooded into the cattle cars, nearly blinding the Jews that were crammed inside. Jacob was grateful for the sudden breath of fresh air. It cleansed his nostrils from the stench of soiling himself, but not his soul from the indignity.

"*Gehen Sie hinaus! Und Hast,*" a German soldier shouted at the Jews packed inside. His car began to empty, but Jacob could not make his legs move. They were numb.

The soldier cracked his whip. "I said move!"

Jacob forced his left leg to go forward, but his right refused. He stumbled and fell. This time, when the whip cracked, the cat-o'-nine-tails landed across Jacob's back, its metal barbs piercing his tweed jacket.

"Can't you see he's sick?" the woman next to him asked. Others quickly warned her to be quiet.

"You two," the soldier pointed, "get him down, his bag too." Some of the younger men lifted Jacob and got him out of the cattle car. "It's two kilometers to Theresienstadt, so don't just stand there. Get going! Move! Move!" the soldier yelled.

Over the two-kilometer hike, as circulation returned to Jacob's lower extremities, his arthritic knees began to throb.

"Form two lines! Women in one, men in the other," ordered a guard inside the gate as they entered the camp. They passed a moat. From there the new arrivals were directed into a treeless courtyard surrounded by yellow and white buildings.

"Men check in on the right, women on the left."

Jacob's line inched ahead very slowly. Standing still for so long in the sun made him feel faint. Somehow, he managed to make it to his next checkpoint without passing out.

"Papers!"

Jacob handed the guard his documents.

"You're a rabbi?"

"I was," Jacob said, not bothering to add that he no longer believed in God.

"Place your valise on the table and open it."

Jacob did as he was told. The guard began rummaging through his belongings. "Any cigarettes? Jewelry?"

"No."

"You won't need this," the guard said, removing a silver frame.

"May I keep the photo?" Jacob asked, knowing he was risking a blow across the face. But the guard removed the picture of Sima and shoved it at him. "Wait over there. You still have to be searched and deloused. Then you'll be assigned to a barracks."

Jacob clutched Sima's image and shuffled to the holding area.

Chapter Twenty-three

George Duckwitz sat in the study of a posh apartment rehearsing what he would say to Prime Minister Per Albin Hansson. If Berlin ever learned of George's trip to Stockholm, his career, and quite possibly his life, would be over. But desperate times called for desperate measures, and for Denmark's Jews these times were perilous.

"Welcome to Sweden, Mr. Duckwitz," Prime Minister Hansson said with his hand extended.

George stood up and shook it vigorously. "Thank you for seeing me on such short notice."

"Ekblad explained the matter was urgent. Please, have a seat. May I get you some tea? Or would you prefer coffee?"

"Neither, but thank you," George said, as the prime minister took a seat behind his desk.

"How about a cigar?" the prime minister asked, opening a humidor.

"I'll have one of my own," George said, reaching into his breast pocket, "but you go ahead."

Both men lit up.

"At the end of the month," George continued, "the Reich will be deporting our Jews to Theresienstadt."

"Are you certain?"

"I'm positive."

"How does that concern me?"

George leaned forward. "Denmark needs your help."

"What can I do?"

"Wire Hitler. Offer to take Denmark's Jews."

The prime minister stared, speechless. "How many Jews are we talking about?"

"Roughly seventy-five hundred."

"All at once?"

"You're their only hope of survival."

The prime minister stared at George in silence for several more seconds. "I can't give you an answer right now."

"When can you give me an answer?" George asked, trying not to show his anxiety. "Time is running out."

"I'll convene an emergency meeting of the cabinet and put the question to them." He glanced at his watch. "Meet me back here at seven."

~*~*~

When Flem entered Liesel's hospital room, his heart stopped. Her bed was empty. Battling fear, he rushed to the nurse's station. "Can you tell me where Liesel Prestur is? She's not in her room."

"Are you a member of her family?"

"We are engaged. Her father, Dr. Prestur, cleared me for visits."

"He left no such instructions with me."

"Are you sure?" Flem asked, refusing to give up.

"Even if he did, visiting hours won't start for another two hours."

"Can you at least tell me how she's doing?"

"I'm afraid that is privileged information. Now, if you'll excuse me, I have a lot of charting I still need to finish."

"Then can you tell me where Mrs. Prestur is?"

"No, I can't," she said, giving him an exasperated look.

"Why are you being so difficult?" Flem asked.

"Is there a problem, Nurse Havass?" a male voice asked from behind him. Flem turned around to see Dr. Colbertsen.

"Liesel isn't in her room," Flem said. "Do you know where they've taken her?"

"I sent her to Radiology a little while ago," the doctor replied.

"Then she is okay?"

"Better than okay. She's regained consciousness. Her mother tried to reach you a few minutes ago, but there was no answer."

"May I see her, Doctor?"

"Absolutely! I'll take you there now, just give me a moment." Dr. Colbertsen leaned over the desk. "If you'll open Miss Prestur's chart, Nurse Havass, you'll find Flem's name on a list of people with visiting privileges."

The nurse's cheeks turned red. "I'm sorry. I didn't know."

Looking stern, Dr. Colbertsen said, "Then you should have asked. This is a hospital, Nurse Havass, not a penal colony."

"Yes, Doctor."

He turned and placed his hand on Flem's shoulder. "It's back this way. Follow me."

"When can she leave the hospital, Doctor?"

"Not for a day or two. We still don't know why she lapsed into a coma in the first place."

"Are you worried that she might relapse?"

Dr. Colbertsen shrugged. "I only practice medicine, Flem. I've not perfected it."

Flem smiled. "Is she in any pain?"

"Except for that lump on the side of her head, she's feeling terrific. Her father is quite relieved."

"He's back?" Flem asked as they turned down another corridor.

"No, and he won't be for a few days. He called a little while ago. He's run into some trouble."

"What kind of trouble?" Flem asked, not liking the sound of it.

"You'll have to ask Mrs. Prestur. She spoke to him after I did," Dr. Colbertsen said as he opened the door to Radiology. Flem spotted Liesel's mother standing next to an orderly. She smiled and opened her arms to him.

"Is Dr. Prestur okay?" he whispered as he hugged her.

147

"We can't talk out here," she said.

"Were you with Liesel when she came to?"

"I was singing her a lullaby."

Flem smiled. "Did she say how the accident happened?"

"She doesn't remember much, Flem. But she'll be back any minute, and you can ask her yourself."

As if on cue, the door on their right swung wide. An orderly backed out, then turned the wheelchair he was pushing around.

Liesel beamed at them.

"Can't you walk?" Flem asked, fearing the worst.

"They won't let me," Liesel said. "Hospital rules."

"Would I be breaking the rules if I wheeled Liesel myself?"

"That should be fine," the orderly said. "Just don't break any speed limits."

"I'll make certain of that," Mrs. Prestur assured him.

With a smile, the orderly stepped aside, and Flem took his place pushing her wheelchair. When they reached the exit, Mrs. Prestur opened the double doors, almost hitting one of two S.S. officers that were about to enter.

The taller one wearing a monocle asked, "Are you Dr. Prestur's wife?"

"I am," she said.

Flem began to pray.

"Then you will have to come with us."

"Where are you taking her?" Liesel asked, turning white.

"Down to Headquarters to be questioned."

"What's this all about?" Flem asked, feeling his mouth go dry.

"And who are you?" the shorter one demanded as he rhythmically struck his blackjack against his palm.

"Fleming Lund. What do you need to question her about?"

"Her husband's whereabouts. Now step aside."

With tears in her eyes, Mrs. Prestur turned to Flem. "Take care of my daughter," she said as they led her away.

Liesel began to weep. Then Dr. Colbertsen came up to them and asked, "What's going on?"

"They're taking Mrs. Prestur in for questioning about her husband," Flem explained.

The doctor's countenance darkened. "We better go to my office. I've something to tell you."

In his office, Dr. Colbertsen asked his nurse to excuse them for a few minutes. When she left, he locked the door. Flem took a seat next to Liesel's wheelchair.

"Your father went to Elsinore," Dr. Colbertsen replied, folding his hands across his blotter.

Flem didn't like the serious expression on the doctor's face.

"He went to consult another doctor about my case," Liesel explained to Flem.

"No, Liesel. That was just a cover story. What I'm about to tell you must remain a secret. Your father, as well as several other doctors here at the hospital, have been helping the Resistance. More than that, I can't tell you. It would be too risky."

"How did the German's find out?" Flem asked, praying it wasn't through Aldur.

Dr. Colbertsen shrugged. "I don't know."

Liesel turned to Flem. "I heard you and Mother talking yesterday. I know you think Aldur informed on Father, but he didn't. I know he didn't! He loves Father. I know he does."

Bewildered, Flem gaped at her. "Just a few days ago, you were telling me how much your brother hated him."

"It's best not to jump to conclusion. It could be anyone," Dr. Colbertsen said. "The Gestapo has informants everywhere. Don't burn any bridges."

~*~*~

When George Duckwitz returned to the prime minister's apartment that evening, his bunions had bunions. Except for the two hours he had spent in a cinema watching lovely Ingrid Bergman play opposite a gruff-looking American with an overbite, George had spent the afternoon on his feet, walking the streets. *Casablanca*, he was certain, would never be shown in Denmark. Its message, that ordinary people could make a difference, was far too subversive for the Reich.

"The prime minister will see you now."

George rose and followed the butler into the library. When the prime minister flashed him a friendly smile, George began to relax.

"Sweden will accept Denmark's Jews, provided Germany approves. Our embassy in Copenhagen will inform you as soon as we hear from Berlin."

Deflated, George boarded the plane back to Denmark. He had done all he could. Now he must wait and pray for a miracle. It would take one of biblical proportions to get Hitler to agree.

Chapter Twenty-four

Aldur ignored the knock, hoping whoever it was would get the message. Instead, the rapping grew more insistent. "Open the door, Aldur. It's Ursula."

"I'm sick. Go away."

"It's ten o'clock in the morning."

"I don't care if it's noon. I need to sleep. Leave me alone!" He rolled over and pulled the covers over his head.

"There's a doctor on the telephone. He wants to talk to you about your sister."

Aldur's head shot up. "I'll be right there."

He was still buttoning his shirt as he raced down the stairs in his stocking feet. In the parlor, Ursula held out the phone to him.

"Hello."

"Aldur, this is Dr. Colbertsen. Could you come down to the hospital right away? Your sister wants to talk to you."

"I'll be right there," he said and hung up the phone. "Run up and get my shoes, will you, Ursula? And my jacket."

She draped her arms around his neck. "Isn't there something you want to do first?"

Then he noticed a brown mark on her neck peeking out above her scarf. Certain that he had not put it there, he kissed her without feeling, knowing it would be the last time. Then he said, "Hurry, please. Liesel wants to talk to me."

"She's better then?"

"Forget it. I'll get them myself." This was the perfect opportunity to pack his things and move back home.

~*~*~

"I'll be in the chapel," Flem told Liesel. "It will be better if I'm not here when Aldur arrives."

"I just don't believe he is capable of something so monstrous."

"Of course you don't. He's your brother. You love him."

"He's struggling, Flem, with God and himself."

"I hope you're right."

"Don't give up on him, Flem. I never gave up on you."

"I'm so glad that you didn't," he said, opening the door.

"Me, too." She blew him a kiss. He went out and closed the door. In the hall, Katlev was walking toward him. "Are you okay?"

"Aldur's on his way here to talk to Liesel," Flem replied, grabbing Katlev's shoulder. "I'll explain everything in the chapel. It's this way. Follow me."

As the sun's rays filtered through the stained glass, casting red and blue beams across the altar, Flem filled Katlev in on everything that had happened.

"Liesel, of course, doesn't believe Aldur had anything to do with it. But I'm not so sure."

"Collaborators are everywhere, Flem. Remember what Sister Superior said? Resistance is a dangerous business. No offense, but Liesel might know her brother better than you do. Besides, haven't you been praying for him?"

Flem rubbed his face. "I'm doing it again, aren't I?"

"Doing what again?" Katlev asked.

"Praying for something to happen, then doubting that it could."

His friend smiled. "Why don't we go down to the altar?"

"Yes, I need to pray for Liesel's father."

"And Aldur."

Flem sighed. "And Aldur."

Miracle Across the Sound

~*~*~

Aldur headed down the corridor taking deep cleansing breaths. When he reached his sister's room, he knocked softly and then opened the door.

Liesel turned from looking out the window and smiled at him.

"Can you ever forgive me?" he asked rushing to her side. "I swear I didn't mean what I said."

Hearing this, his sister's smile faded.

"I would do anything, Liesel, if I could take it all back. Please believe me!"

"What did you say?...And to whom did you say it?"

"To you, of course, just before the accident."

"Oh, thank God!" she said and visibly relaxed.

"What did you think I meant?"

"The Gestapo just took Mother in for questioning."

Aldur's heart began to pound. "Mother? Did they arrest Father too?"

"Not that I know of, but he's in some kind of trouble in Elsinore."

"I was afraid of this," Alder said. He ran his fingers through his hair, trying to think.

"What do you know about it, Aldur? The cleaning woman told Mother you were hiding in Father's office."

"I wasn't hiding...not at first. I went there to write an apology." He took hold of her hands. "You have to believe me, Liesel. I know I've been a jerk, but I had nothing to do with Mother's arrest."

"Then why did you say you were afraid this might happen?"

"I overheard Father tell her he was going to Elsinore to help the Resistance." When tears pooled in his sister's eyes, he wiped them away. "I wish I could stay with you, Liesel, but I have to find Father."

"Then please, take Flem with you! He's in the chapel."

"Pray for us, will you?"

"I have been...and I will."

Aldur kissed her and left.

153

~*~*~

Flem was on his knees when the door behind him opened. He turned to see who had come in.

"Liesel told me I would find you here," Aldur said, approaching him. "I need to speak to you in private."

"Anything you have to say to me, you can say in front of Katlev," Flem told him, getting up. Katlev rose too.

"I'm going to Elsinore to find my father. Liesel thought you might want to go with me."

Was this a trap? Flem wondered, not ready to trust him.

"Look," Aldur said, "there's something you should know. It might help you decide."

"Go on, I'm listening," Flem said.

Aldur lowered his head. "I heard you praying in here yesterday. I was resting on a pew when you came in."

"That was you?"

Alder lowered his head again. "Earlier my mother accused me of not having a soul. I can't tell you everything now," he said raising it again to make eye contact, "but I want you to know that I'm sorry for the way I've been acting."

Flashing Katlev a smile, Flem shouted, "Well, hallelujah!" then extended his hand to his future brother-in-law.

Aldur gripped it tightly. "We better get going."

"Not so fast!" Katlev said grasping each of their shoulders. "We must pray first, then pay Sister Superior a visit."

~*~*~

In a private car with the shades pulled, Flem filled Aldur in on the extra-curricular activities taking place at the cloister in Elsinore.

"You might want to drop me off some place first," Aldur suggested.

"But you're Dr. Prestur's son," Flem said.

"And a card-carrying Nazi," Aldur reminded him.

"I'd tear that up now, if I were you."

"The boy has a point," Katlev said. "Sister Superior already knows us. We can drop him off at the tavern and pick him up after we speak to the nuns."

"Good idea," Flem said, "but we will need a cover story in case we are questioned."

"Why not tell the truth?" Katlev suggested. "We went to Elsinore to find Dr. Prestur because his wife was picked up for questioning."

"What about the colleague he's supposed to be there to consult?" Flem asked.

"Elsinore must have a doctor," Aldur said. "All we have to do to establish our alibi is pay him a visit."

"And what do we do when he says he doesn't know your father?" Flem asked.

"We only need to show that we're there to find my father. When we do, I'm sure he'll have a cover story of his own."

"Before we drop you off, we need to rent some bicycles," Katlev said. "We just need to make sure we aren't seen taking the road to the convent."

Chapter Twenty-five

Theresienstadt Concentration Camp

Jacob took a sip of what was supposed to be coffee and immediately spit it out. "What is this stuff?" he asked.

"Ersatz coffee," the man sitting next to him said.

Jacob eyed the loaf of black bread on their table. Before the war, a loaf that size would've fed two. Here, it was used to starve six. They should have just shot me, Jacob thought, watching the pitiful creatures at his table shoveling in crumbs.

In Germany, Jacob rarely went hungry thanks to the farmer who hid him. Potatoes, turnips, apples, and an occasional piece of fish, had kept him sated. Not like in the old days, of course, when he ate only the best kosher food. Those days ended in November of '38. Now Jacob wondered if they ever existed. What if they were a dream and this the reality?

A bell began clanging. "Time to work!" a guard shouted into a megaphone. All the prisoners stood and formed two lines.

"Come with me," a guard ordered as Jacob was about to exit the mess. Knowing better than to ask where, Jacob followed him. They passed several buildings in silence, then entered Camp Headquarters. Inside, another guard escorted Jacob to an office at the end of a long hall and ordered him to sit. Several minutes later, the major behind the desk called Jacob's name.

156

"I've been reviewing your papers and have decided to keep you here. A vacancy has come up in the Altestenrat that you can fill."

"What's the Altestenrat?"

"The Jewish Council," the officer explained, opening a drawer. He pulled out a sheet of paper, stamped it, then held it out to Jacob. "Take this to Sudeten Barracks. Give it to Edelstein. He will explain your duties."

"My duties?"

"Work, you stupid Jew! You're not here on vacation. Now, get going!"

~*~*~

Flem straddled his bicycle and glanced over his shoulder. A large brown hare twitched its nose then scampered into the field on the deserted backroad. Satisfied no one was watching, he said, "Let's go."

Seven or eight minutes later, they reached the convent, only to find a black Mercedes parked in front of the cloister's doors.

"Now what do we do?" Flem asked.

"Follow me," Katlev said and headed into the wooded area to their left. After camouflaging their bikes with some branches, they got down on their stomachs and waited. Ten minutes later, two S.S. men came out. Mother Superior followed them to their car.

"Contact Headquarters immediately if anything suspicious happens."

"We're a law-abiding order. We know what our duty is."

"Knowing it is one thing, doing it is another. Heil Hitler!"

"Heil Hitler," the nun responded.

As soon as the Mercedes rounded the bend in the road and disappeared, Mother Superior made the sign of the cross.

Flem helped Katlev to his feet.

"We need to talk to you, Sister," Katlev called out as she was about to go back into the convent.

The nun spun around. "Hurry! You must get inside. It's much too dangerous out here." In less than a minute they were all safely behind the cloister's double doors.

"I don't want to be disturbed unless Quick Silver shows up or the S.S. returns," Mother Superior told one of her nuns.

"Sister Theresa is in the tower keeping watch."

"Splendid. Take everyone else into the chapel and have them pray."

~*~*~

Finishing his drink, Aldur looked around the smoke-filled tavern, wishing he had spent more time reading Sherlock Holmes novels as a kid. He might have picked up a few tricks.

"Would you like a refill?" the innkeeper asked him as he wiped down the bar.

"What I'd like is some information."

The man stopped wiping. "This isn't a library. What do you want to know?"

"I'm looking for my father, Dr. Prestur. He came here yesterday, to Elsinore, I mean, not necessarily this establishment." After several seconds of an intense stare, the bartender began wiping the bar again. "He came here to consult a colleague about my sister," Aldur went on when it became clear that the tavernkeeper wasn't going to comment. "The problem is I don't know who this colleague was. So, I was hoping you might give me the names of the doctors who practice here in Elsinore."

"We had one doctor here in Elsinore," a man at a table behind Aldur said. Aldur turned around to see who was addressing him. "But he won't be consulting with anyone anymore thanks to the Germans."

"That's enough, Edvard!" the tavernkeeper warned. "We don't want any trouble!"

"I'm only speaking the truth." Edvard slammed down his empty glass, pulled two coins out of his pocket, dropped them on the table, got up and staggered toward the door.

"Stupid drunk talks too much," the tavernkeeper mumbled.

Maybe so, Aldur thought, but that might not be such a bad thing. Determined to find out if Edvard knew anything about his father,

Aldur threw money on the bar to cover his drink and a generous tip, then hurried after him. But he was too late. The drunk was already halfway down the road, weaving from one side to the other.

He could hop on his bike and catch up to him, only he had promised Flem that he would wait for them here at the tavern. Frustrated, Aldur went back inside.

The chambermaid was whispering into the tavernkeeper's ear, but their conversation stopped as soon as they noticed Aldur. She straightened her dust cap then hurried toward the stairs.

The tavernkeeper disappeared into the supply room behind the bar, then came out in less than a minute. He drew a fresh glass of lager and set it down in front of Aldur. "This one is on me."

"Thanks," Aldur said, a little suspicious of his generosity. Maintaining eye contact, he set a napkin down on the bar in front of Aldur, on which someone had printed: Wait at the bottom of the fire escape in back of the tavern.

Zapped with adrenalin, Aldur glanced around. No one was watching. He folded the napkin and slipped it into his jacket. "I'm expecting a couple of friends at any time. If they show up before I come back, please ask them to wait."

"Certainly," the innkeeper said.

Outside, Aldur lit a cigarette, hoping it would settle his nerves, but the odds that this was a setup was slim. Most Danes would cut off a finger if they could stick it in the eye of a German, Aldur mused, rounding the side of the tavern. When he reached the fire escape, he spotted a small rock with a slip of paper under it on one of the steps. He picked it up. Second floor, third door to the left, the note said. He shoved it into his pocket and started his ascent.

~*~*~

Flem noticed the strain on Mother Superior's face as she bid him and Katlev to take a seat.

"A collaborator tipped off the Gestapo. They raided one of the safe houses and killed several members of the Resistance."

"Was Dr. Prestur one of them?" Flem asked.

"The doctor escaped. His patients weren't that fortunate. The owner of the house has been arrested."

"Where is Dr. Prestur now?" Flem asked.

"A leader in the Underground, a man called Quick Silver, telephoned us a little while ago."

"Isn't that dangerous?" Katlev asked.

"We use a code for these matters," the nun explained. "Dr. Prestur took a bullet. Quick Silver took him to a place where he'll be safe for now, but he can only remain there a day. Any longer will put too many others at risk."

"Does the Gestapo know Dr. Prestur's identity?" Katlev asked.

"We aren't sure. We don't yet know who the collaborator is."

Flem's stomach knotted. "Where was Dr. Prestur wounded?"

"I don't know that either," the nun said.

"Dr. Prestur's wife was taken in for questioning about her husband's whereabouts earlier this morning, so they must know something," Flem said.

Mother Superior made the sign of the cross. "We've been praying novenas to the Blessed Mother every night and will continue to do so."

Flem and Katlev exchanged frowns, but this was no time to get into a theological debate about an act of idolatry. So biting his tongue, Flem asked, "How is the gunnery sergeant?"

"He and what's left of his crew are on a submarine bound for Britain as we speak."

"Well, that's one less thing to worry about," Katlev said.

Flem continued to frown, consumed with what they would do with Dr. Prestur once they found him. "We can't take Dr. Prestur home wounded. He'll have to go into hiding."

"I'll find someone who can smuggle him into Sweden," Mother Superior assured them.

"I can do it," Katlev said. "I can take Dr. Prestur and his wife once the Gestapo releases her."

"How soon do you expect to hear from Quick Silver?" Flem asked.

160

"I don't know." Mother Superior opened her desk drawer. She removed a pad and pen, then shoved them toward Flem. "Give me your address. I'll send a message once I know more."

"What if Dr. Prestur isn't stable enough to make the trip?" Flem asked.

Katlev laid a hand on Flem's arm. "The crossing only takes a few hours. Don't borrow trouble, my boy."

"How many will be making this trip?" the nun asked.

"Flem's parents, his cousin, that's three," Katlev replied. "Dr. and Mrs. Prestur, Liesel and possibly her brother—seven all together, if Aldur plans to leave too."

"What about you?" Flem asked.

"You will need to dock your boat here in Elsinore," Mother Superior said. "That way you'll be ready to sail at a moment's notice."

"When I return, could I stay in one of your safe houses?" Katlev asked.

"When you return?" Mother Superior looked confused. "Surely you're not coming back. You're a Jew!"

"God needs me here."

Flem suddenly felt sick. He had promised the old man he would stay and help him, and he promised Liesel that he would go.

"Aren't you afraid?" the nun asked.

"Perfect love casts out fear," Katlev replied.

Mother Superior made another sign of the cross then stood. "You should leave. The way things have been going today, the Gestapo might return at any moment."

Chapter Twenty-six

Aldur looked up and down the dim hallway. The stench of ammonia, or maybe bleach, permeated the air. He read the note again. It said to go to the third room on the left. He made his way there, glanced in both directions, then tapped at the door. A moment later, the chambermaid he'd seen earlier opened it. She stepped aside to let him in then quickly locked up again.

His father lay in a four-poster bed with a bloodstained bandage around his chest. "You've been shot. Is it serious?"

"It won't be, once you get the bullet out."

"Me? I'm not a doctor!"

"I can talk you through it."

As Aldur stared at the bloodstains, his hands began to sweat. "It's near your heart. Can't you find a nurse?"

"For now, you're all I have. How did you find me, anyway? But first tell me about your sister."

"She's fine," Aldur said, wondering how much he should reveal.

"What aren't you telling me?"

"Mother was taken in for questioning right after you phoned the hospital."

His father's already pallid complexion paled further.

"Where is the phone?" Aldur asked, wanting to call Flem.

"It's down the hall, past the stairwell," the chambermaid said. "Ivan helped him make the call."

162

"Who's Ivan?" Aldur asked.

"He's gathering the supplies we'll need to remove the bullet."

"Where is my father's medical bag? It has everything you'll need in it."

"The Germans have it. I told your mother what happened. Didn't she tell you?"

"She was taken away before I got to the hospital. I was in your office yesterday when you and Mother came in. That's how I knew you were in Elsinore."

"You were eavesdropping?"

"I was in there writing you an apology. So much has changed, Father. I moved out of Ursula's this morning before going to the hospital."

"What about your politics? Has that changed too?" his father asked laboring for breath.

"You're a Nazi!" the chambermaid exclaimed, looking horrified.

"Not anymore!" Aldur said. "We came here to help once we heard that you were in trouble."

"Whose 'we'?" his father asked.

"Flem and Katlev. They went to the convent but should be back any time. You told Mother to tell whoever asked where you were to say you were consulting a colleague about Liesel. I've been downstairs establishing that alibi."

"All the alibis in the world won't help him now," the chambermaid said with a frown.

"What do you mean?" Aldur asked.

"They have my bag," his father said then started coughing. Aldur's heart sank. He'd had his father's name engraved on his medical bag as a birthday present two years ago.

~*~*~

From his office window, George Duckwitz watched the boats bobbing in the harbor. He hoped the view would calm him, but it didn't. Only news that Berlin had accepted Sweden's offer could do that, and so far, he'd heard nothing.

What a fool he'd been not to realize this day would come. Hitler's plan to remove Jews from Germany's economic, political, and social life began in 1933. The first time George read *Mein Kampf* he should've realized Der Führer's plan could only end with the removal of every Jew from every German-occupied land.

George lit a cigarette, but the tobacco did nothing to mask the taste of death in his mouth. Then his intercom buzzed.

"Excuse me, Herr Duckwitz. Your wife is on the telephone. Shall I put her through?"

"Why not?" George said. After all, he was only killing time.

~*~*~

Edelstein shoved a clipboard into Jacob's hand. "You will be in charge of our four crematoria."

"Then it's true?" Jacob said and quickly lowered his voice. "We're being exterminated?"

Edelstein stared back with vacant eyes. "Not here. Here we wait and wish we were dead."

"But four crematoria? Who are they burning?"

"Jews that die from natural causes. If being starved and forced to live in unsanitary conditions can be classified as natural. At least our names aren't on rosters for Auschwitz, Dachau, or Buchenwald. For that we can be grateful."

Jacob grabbed Edelstein's wrist. "Lower your voice! There's a guard outside the door! Remember that a man who lacks restraint is like a city with the walls torn down!"

"Don't quote Scripture to me, Rabbi!" Edelstein pulled his arm away. "Not here! Not in this hellhole! You rabbis are all alike. You think you can quote Scripture and make desperate situations better. But you can't!"

"Forgive me," Jacob said. "But we must get back to work. They gave me only twenty minutes for orientation."

Miracle Across the Sound

~*~*~

When Flem and Katlev returned to the Inn, Aldur informed them of all he had learned. They were delighted that Dr. Prestur was there, but Ivan had not yet returned with the supplies needed to remove the bullet. So Flem and Katlev arranged to take a room for the night. During a phone call Flem placed to the hospital, Liesel informed him that her mother was to be transferred to Vestre Prison the following afternoon. Ivan returned with the supplies, shortly after Flem hung up, only to be redeployed to arrange for Mrs. Prestur's escape. The bullet was successfully removed around 8 p.m. At 11 p.m., Ivan returned with word that the Resistance would ambush the vehicle that would be transferring Mrs. Prestur to Vestre Prison on a deserted strip of road twelve kilometers from the prison.

"Let's go over this one more time," Ivan said. "The three of you are to take the 6 a.m. train back to Copenhagen. Aldur, you are to check your sister out of the hospital and take the noon train back here. Flem, you are to collect your family and take them to Katlev's cutter. He will bring them here. I'll disguise Dr. Prestur and have him wait in the car while I pick you and your sister up at the station, then I'll drive them to the boat. We will have to wait there until Mrs. Prestur arrives. Any questions?"

Chapter Twenty-seven

$\mathcal{D}$eidre Prestur gasped when she heard what sounded like a blast. The vehicle began weaving, then slowed, thumping to a stop. Then gunfire erupted. Seconds later, the back of the van opened.

"Don't be afraid," a man with a rifle said as a lorry pulled up behind them. "We are here to take you to your husband. But we must hurry. A German patrol will be passing this way in ten minutes."

~*~*~

George Duckwitz stopped pacing and pulled out his pocket watch. It was almost six. Time had run out. The ships would reach Copenhagen in a few more hours. He must act now. Slipping his timepiece back into his pocket, he turned to his wife. "I have to go out."

"Supper is almost on the table."

"I won't be long," he assured her, taking his overcoat out of the closet. "There is something I must do."

"My roast will be ruined," she complained as he donned his fedora. "Can't it wait?

"I've already waited too long."

"What's gotten into you, George?"

"It's called a conscience," he said and kissed her on the cheek.

"Well, I don't like it! I don't like it one bit. The way you have been acting lately makes me nervous."

"Pour yourself some schnapps," he told her as he headed for the door.

She grabbed his arm. "Promise me you won't do anything crazy, that you won't get us arrested!"

"I'll try my best."

~*~*~

As Ivan led Liesel's mother down the steps into the cabin where Flem's parents and Katlev were waiting, Liesel barely recognized her. Her mother's right eye was black and swollen, her right cheek bruised. Blood stained her blouse.

"Dear God," her father said, pulling her into his arms. "What have they done to you?"

"Are you in pain?" Liesel asked.

"Not much," her mother said. "Where can I wash up?"

"I brought you some clean clothes," Aldur said.

"Thank you," she told him, opening her arms. "You have no idea how glad I am to see you, Son."

"You have no idea how glad I am to be here," Aldur replied, embracing her, "and to hear you call me your son."

"You've found your soul, haven't you?"

"I certainly hope so, Mother."

She patted his cheek, smiling. "You have, Aldur. You have."

"We're all proud of you," his father said. "You have the makings not only of a decent human being but a fine doctor. Your hands were as steady as any surgeon's."

Liesel squeezed her brother's cheek. "Aldur, you're a peach!"

"And a great spy," Katlev added.

"I can vouch for that," Flem said. "Aldur is the one who found your husband."

Liesel knew she would treasure this moment forever, in spite of her future father-in-law looking so lost.

"Well, my boy," Katlev said, laying a hand on Flem's shoulder, "we better get underway. Sweden awaits."

~*~*~

When he reached the Worker's Assembly House on 22 Roemer Street, George Duckwitz stopped to catch his breath before running up the steps. In the main meeting hall, he spotted Hans Hedtoft, head of the Social Democrats.

He hurried over to him. "The disaster is upon us. In a few hours, German ships will anchor in the harbor. At midnight tomorrow, they'll start rounding up the Jews."

"Are you certain?" Hedtoft asked.

"They must go into hiding now."

"But Werner Best assured me this would not happen."

"Best is a liar! Spread the word!" George turned and left the meeting hall with his conscience now cleared.

~*~*~

Hans Hedtoft banged the gavel. "Please, gentlemen, come to order! We have an emergency. I want all my committee heads in my office immediately. I need the rest of you to remain in this room, but our meeting is officially adjourned."

Hedtoft dropped his gavel and hurried into his chamber. Within minutes, the other leaders joined him.

"What's going on?" Hansen asked.

"What we've feared has come to pass. Or it will in a little over twenty-four hours," Hedtoft said, then relayed everything Duckwitz had told him.

"I can't believe this is actually happening."

"Well believe it," Hedtoft said. "Now, I have to go and start warning people. Who wants to come with me?"

Hansen raised his hand.

"The rest of you spread the word. Alert every Jew you know and every non-Jew you can trust."

Chapter Twenty-eight

———

Flem looked up at the night sky. It was lit with a thousand stars.

"I can't stop thinking of Jacob," Katlev said. "I see his face sometimes before I fall asleep."

"Stop beating yourself up."

"He was my best friend, and I failed him. What's more, I failed the Lord."

"Ha Shem has forgiven you. Let it go!"

"It won't let me go," Katlev said, about to untie the boat, when Flem noticed someone running toward them down the dock.

"Wait!" Flem said, pointing toward the shadowy figure. "It's Ivan."

"I'm glad I caught you," Ivan said, out of breath. "They're going to round up the Jews tomorrow at midnight."

"On Rosh Hashanah?" Flem said.

"The head of German shipping informed Hans Hedtoft this afternoon."

"Thanks for letting us know." Flem turned to Katlev. "We better shove off."

"Wait!" Ivan said, still trying to catch his breath. "I have a family that needs to go with you."

"How soon can they get here?" Katlev asked.

"They're in my car now."

When Katlev nodded, Ivan dashed off and returned a moment later. "This is Martin Cohen," Ivan announced, straightening the four-year-old's cap.

"Introductions can wait until we're underway," Katlev said, lifting the toddler into the boat as his mother boarded, carrying his infant brother. "I can fit four adults and two of the children in the bulkhead. The rest of you will have to hide under the tarps in cargo."

"What about the wheelhouse?" Flem asked.

"There's not enough room," Katlev said.

Mrs. Prestur sighed. "Let's just pray we won't be stopped."

"If we're boarded and they have dogs, we can use this," Dr. Prestur said, removing a balled-up handkerchief from his jacket. "This powder will temporarily deaden a dog's sense of smell."

"Where did you get it?" Flem asked.

"A scientist in the Underground developed it using cocaine and dried blood. I'll sprinkle some around if it looks like we're about to be boarded."

~*~*~

Flem noticed the spring in Katlev's step. Smuggling people to freedom had given the old man new purpose, a purpose Flem wanted so much to share, but how could he without disappointing Liesel?

"I must speak to you."

Recognizing Aldur's voice, Flem turned around.

"In private. What I need to tell you can't be overheard."

"That sounds ominous," Flem said. "Follow me."

When they reached the engine room, Flem opened the door and let Aldur enter first.

"I'm joining the Underground."

"Are you crazy?" Flem exclaimed. "You'll be arrested for sure."

"Not if I play my cards right."

"Your father's a wanted man."

"And as far as the Reich's concerned, I'm a card-carrying Nazi. The Party holds the documentation to prove it."

"I don't know, Aldur…"

"Look, Katlev will already be in hiding. So, I can report him for smuggling all of you to Sweden. It will convince the Germans that I'm on their side. Besides, Ursula's father will vouch for me. I'm sure of it."

"I thought you two broke up."

"That's easily rectified."

"I don't know, Aldur. It sounds pretty dangerous."

"Have you seen my mother's back? Those pigs whipped her, Flem! I have to do this. You can't talk me out of it."

Flem drew in a deep breath, then placed a hand on Aldur's shoulder. "I do understand. And thank you!"

"For what?"

"Helping me make up my mind. I've decided to go back with Katlev. I just don't know how to tell your sister."

"We could tell her together," Aldur suggested, "and my parents, too."

~*~*~

Everyone was in the cabin except Katlev who was at the helm, keeping his eyes peeled for Germans.

Flem cleared his throat. "May I have your attention? Aldur and I have a few announcements to make."

"I better go first," Aldur said. "I'm joining the Underground. I'm letting all of you know now, so I don't have to waste time when we reach our destination."

Aldur's mother covered her mouth. Her audible gasp broke Flem's heart, but it was Liesel's rage that shocked him.

"Vengeance belongs to God, Aldur!" his sister said.

"You saw what they did to Mother, Liesel!" Aldur exclaimed with equal vehemence.

"You'll get yourself killed!" she warned him.

"What was your other announcement?" Mrs. Prestur asked, stepping between them.

"I'm returning with Katlev," Flem said, "to help others escape."

Chapter Twenty-nine

As whispers of the raid spread throughout Copenhagen, nearly everyone got involved. Those unable to leave work called friends. Many went through the phone book, looking for Jewish names, so they could warn them. Almost everyone with an attic, a basement, a boathouse, or an extra room took someone in. Many took in whole families, never giving a thought to how they would ever smuggle them across the Sound into Sweden.

When Olga Barfeldt hung up the phone, she immediately called James Margolinsky, a Jew whom she knew had many contacts in the community. "I must speak to you immediately, but not on the telephone. I'm coming right over."

Several minutes later, Margolinsky opened his door.

"I'm not staying long. I just came to warn you. At midnight tomorrow, they will start arresting Jews. You must warn as many as you can and go into hiding."

"How do you know this?"

"I just got a call."

"But are you sure?"

"Who can be sure of anything these days? But why take a chance?"

It was almost curfew when Margolinsky shut the door. First thing in the morning he would go to the synagogue and warn the rabbi, then go see his friend who owned a beach house up the coast. Fritz was a Lutheran, but Margolinsky was certain he would help.

172

~*~*~

The rabbi's sense that something was wrong was confirmed when Margolinsky whispered the grim news into his ear. Like a sleepwalker, he made his way down the aisle of his synagogue.

"You all must leave immediately. Return to your homes. Go and warn your families. Warn every Jew you know. Instruct them to hide. The raid will begin at midnight."

"But tonight's Rosh Hashanah!" one of the Minyan exclaimed. "Are you certain of this, Rabbi?"

"Yes! Go! Get out of here!"

When the prayer hall had emptied, the rabbi rushed to his office and picked up the phone. With a shaking hand, he dialed the number for his old friend from childhood. After a few rings, Pastor Kildeby answered the phone.

"Thank God you are home," the rabbi said. "It's happening. At midnight tonight it will begin."

"Then you must come at once," Pastor Kildeby said. "I can put three rooms at your disposal."

"If you're caught, you know what will happen."

There was a short pause. Then his old friend said, "Well, I won't be the first to face prison for doing the Lord's work, so hurry!"

With a lump in his throat, the rabbi returned the receiver to its cradle and dialed the number for the Lutheran church down the street from his synagogue.

"We have an emergency."

"I'll be right over," the pastor replied.

~*~*~

Katlev, Aldur, and Flem slept on the boat when they returned from Copenhagen but were up by five the next morning. "You must be careful," Flem said, shaking Aldur's hand. "You know what will happen if your Nazi friends begin to suspect you."

"If I need to get word to you, I'll contact the Elsinore Sewing Group," Aldur replied—code for the Underground.

Flem nodded his understanding. "Just remember that Sweden is only a short boat ride away if things get too hot."

"A boat ride through German-patrolled waters," Katlev reminded them. "But the Lord will be your rearguard," he told Aldur. He hugged him goodbye then turned to Flem. "Well, we better get moving. The Lord has work for us to do."

~*~*~

"Thank you for coming," the rabbi said, greeting the young minister. "I've just been informed that the Gestapo will begin arresting Jews tonight."

"I was afraid of this, but don't worry. I will make a few calls and arrange a place for you and your family to hide until we can get you out of the country."

"Thank you, but that's been taken care of. There's something else, equally important, I hope you will be able to do for me."

"Of course. What is it?"

"Can you hide our Torah scroll and a few other valuables?"

"Why certainly! Our church has a large cellar. Your relics will be safe until you return."

The rabbi choked back tears. "You mean *if* we return, don't you?"

The young minister clasped the rabbi's shoulder. "No, Rabbi, I mean when you return. Rest assured that our people will help your people in every way we can. I'll go back now and get my wheelbarrow and some blankets."

~*~*~

An ambulance driver on his way to work noticed two of his neighbors with their heads together whispering. Their expressions looked grim. Having a few minutes to spare, he went over to find out what was wrong.

"Haven't you heard?"

"Heard what?"

His neighbor crooked her finger.

He lowered his head, and she cupped her mouth to his ear. "They're going to start rounding up the Jews at midnight. The ships are in the harbor. You must tell everyone you know. I'm on my way to warn my dentist. My cousin has a summer place in Rungsted and is willing to take in all six of them."

"I'm going to the fish market!" his other neighbor said, then turned and hurried down the sidewalk.

"You must warn everyone you trust at the hospital."

"Yes, I suppose, I can do that," he said, then got a better idea. He ran back to his apartment and called his supervisor. "Something has come up. I won't be in today."

"Are you sick?" she asked.

He lowered his voice to a whisper. "You know those rumors we've been hearing? Well, the ships are in the harbor. Tell everyone concerned. They need to be gone by midnight."

When the ambulance driver hung up, he grabbed his phone directory and slipped it inside of his overcoat. Down in the garage, in his ambulance, he began looking up names that sounded Jewish. He would pay as many as possible a visit. Those with no one to turn to, he would take to the hospital. He knew of three, possibly four, physicians who would be willing to hide them.

~*~*~

01 October, 1943

Word of the roundup had spread throughout the country like wildfire. Only the few who were unwilling to believe an atrocity of this magnitude could happen in Denmark remained in their homes. Those too old or too sick to escape waited in fear. Everyone else went into hiding. Many of them were sheltered by total strangers, ordinary Danes who refused to let evil triumph.

When Werner Best awoke on October 1, he knew he had a problem.

"What do you mean you've only arrested two hundred?"

"They were gone. Disappeared! Vanished!"

"On Rosh Hashanah?" Best bellowed, beginning to sweat. How would he explain this to Berlin? He had already sent them a telegram proclaiming that Denmark was *JUDENREIN*! Free of Jews! Purged!

"We will keep searching, of course, Herr Best."

"See that you do that." Best gave the salute.

The moment the officer left, Best rushed over to his credenza and poured himself a schnapps. Door after door had been kicked in, but very few Jews had been rounded up. He'd be a laughingstock if the S.S. didn't turn this disaster around quickly. Then it occurred to him what he must do. After draining his glass, he returned to his desk and pressed the intercom. "I need you to take a letter."

"I'll be right in," his secretary told him.

A minute later, Best began his dictation. "We will immediately begin releasing interned Danes, in exchange for information about Jews that are in hiding."

His secretary peered over her glasses. "Is that all?"

"For now," Best said, pleased with his strategy.

"To whom shall I send this?"

"To the press. It's to be the headline in every Danish newspaper. Then call all the radio stations and have them announce it every hour, on the hour."

"Right away, sir," she said, getting up.

"I should be back in a few hours. If you need me before then, you can reach me at Vestre Prison. I must advise General Gørtz and Vice Admiral Vedel about this in person."

~*~*~

Niels Bohr remained adamant. "I don't care! I'm not leaving Sweden until this matter is concluded."

"But Niels," begged Professor Fredrick Lindemann, Churchill's personal consultant in scientific matters, "the plane is waiting. You must fly to London. That was our agreement. It's why we had you smuggled out of Denmark."

"I'm aware of why I'm here, but this must take precedence."

"Why are you worrying about Jews when Hitler could develop

the atom bomb at any moment? Tyranny will rule the planet! Is that what you want?"

Unmoved by the diatribe, Niels donned his spectacles. "What I want is an audience with King Gustav. I'm not leaving Sweden until I get it." Niels picked up his newspaper.

"But you've already met with the foreign minister. What more can you do?"

"Yes, and it was a waste of time. I must speak to the king."

"But Einstein is expecting you in Manhattan in two days."

"He can wait," Niels told him.

"But you can't! We can't protect you here. Every hour you delay you are putting yourself at risk. You could be kidnapped, or even assassinated! You have to leave Stockholm!"

"Then get me the king. Those are my terms."

"I'll see what I can do." Professor Lindemann turned on his heels and stormed out of the room.

The next day, Niels rose when the king entered his conference room. "Thank you for granting me this audience, Your Highness."

"I've been informed that you are quite a stubborn fellow," the king said, taking a seat at the head of the table.

"What I am, Your Highness, is a Dane and half Jewish. I owe it to my countrymen to do everything I can."

"And a renowned scientist, which I suppose allows you the privilege of stomping your feet when you don't get your way."

"Would you prefer that I hold my breath?" Niels asked, returning the king's smile.

"Certainly not. Just sit down and make your case."

"Offer asylum to Denmark's Jews," Niels said, still standing.

"I already have. Germany turned us down."

"Forget Germany! Announce it to Denmark! To the world! Run it as a headline in every Swedish paper."

The king remained silent for several seconds. "You certainly know how to make demands."

"It's a request, and I'm not finished."

"Why am I not surprised?"

"I want you to broadcast it into Denmark every hour. The Jews must be assured they have a haven to which they can flee."

"Hitler would be furious. We're supposed to be neutral."

"Damn Hitler! And damn neutrality! *You* are the king of Sweden."

Another pause ensued, one longer than the first. Noticing the king's jaw clinch, Niels feared he'd pressed too hard. He was about to apologize when the king stood up.

"Very well. Consider it done."

~*~*~

At a small table in a downtown café in Copenhagen, Aldur pulled out a chair across from Ursula's father. "Sorry I'm late," he said as he sat down, but Mr. Grund did not return his smile. "Traffic is unbearable with all the extra troops in town. Have you noticed?"

"They're searching for Jews and members of the Underground."

Aldur folded his hands. "Yes, I've heard. One of them is my father. I'll never be able to hold my head up again."

Mr. Grund looked at him skeptically. "We're here to talk about my daughter. My wife and I opened our home to you. We accepted you as one of the family."

"For which I'm grateful, but did you see the marks on her neck?"

"What are you talking about?"

"I didn't put them there," Aldur said.

Mr. Grund's face turned red.

"I'm in love with her," Aldur continued, "but not willing to share her with every German in uniform. After all, a man has his pride."

Ursula's father remained silent for a moment. Aldur couldn't tell if he was furious or devastated.

"You leave her to me," Mr. Grund finally said. He lifted his glass. "This won't happen again. Come to dinner tomorrow night."

One problem was solved, but Aldur couldn't relax. Now he had another.

Chapter Thirty

Montreal, Canada

Henrik Kauffmann, Denmark's ambassador to the United States, shoved the wire he'd just read into his breast pocket. "Please excuse me," he told the mayor, rising from the table. "Something has come up that I must deal with right away."

"Is there something I can do?"

"Pray!" he said heading for the exit. "Our Jews are being deported."

In his hotel room an hour later, Kauffmann read the letter he had written, to make sure it had set the right tone.

I just received word that our German occupiers have begun deportation of Denmark's Jews. I can do little from here to aid my fellow citizens, except to request that your government undertake immediate humanitarian measures to aid our Jewish population.

I guarantee reimbursement from Denmark's public funds, which are under my control in the United States, for any expenses your government might incur to aid our persecuted nationals, fully assured that the Danish people will back me up.

Satisfied with what he'd written, Kauffmann folded his letter and placed it in an envelope addressed to the U.S. Secretary of State. Next, he cabled the Swedish foreign minister, assuring him that Denmark would underwrite all costs incurred assisting Danish refugees. That done, he began telephoning prominent Jewish American leaders.

Back in Washington D. C., two days later, Kauffmann received a telegram from the German-controlled Danish government, demanding that he return to Denmark immediately and stand trial for treason.

He picked up the phone. "This is Henrik Kauffmann, Ambassador to Denmark. I need to speak to the president."

"I'll have to ring you back," the operator told him.

Twenty minutes later, the President of the United States returned his call.

"You did the right thing," President Roosevelt assured him. "Don't worry. I'll have Congress recognize you as the official representative of Free Denmark."

"Thank you, Mr. President. You have no idea what a relief that is. If there is anything I can do to repay you, you have only to ask."

"There is something you could do, just until the war ends. You can grant the United States authority over Greenland."

"Mr. President, consider it done."

"Splendid. I will let Cordell Hull know as soon as I hang up. He'll have Congress pass a bill putting all Danish funds in our country at your disposal."

Kauffmann smiled. That would give him nearly twenty million to help the Jews. "Thank you, sir. Hitler will be apoplectic."

"In that case," the President said, chuckling, "why don't we add part of the Danish National Bank's gold stock. Maybe it will kill the scoundrel, and we can end this damn war early."

~*~*~

Helsingborg Sweden
02 October, 1943

With barely enough room to stand in the crowded soup kitchen, Liesel was glad she wasn't really hungry. Nearly every table was filled to capacity with refugees from Copenhagen. A few faces Liesel knew.

Others looked familiar. Most, like the haggard-looking mother trying to drink coffee and sooth her squalling infant, were total strangers.

"May I hold her for you?" Liesel offered.

"That's very kind of you, but I don't want to impose. My husband should be back soon. He went to get a paper."

"It won't be an imposition, I assure you," Liesel said.

"Well, if you're certain, I would like to finish my coffee before it gets cold. I didn't get much sleep last night."

"Take your time." Liesel smiled and extended her arms to accept the tearful bundle. "It's so noisy in here. Would it be okay if I take her outside for a while? It might quiet her down. She is a girl, isn't she?" Liesel asked noting her pink outfit.

"Her name is Greta. You better take this if you're going outside." The woman reached into a bag on the floor next to her chair, pulled out a blanket, and handed it to Liesel.

"We won't be out long," Liesel promised, then spotted her father maneuvering his way through the crowd toward them as she wrapped little Greta snugly.

"This is my father, Dr. Prestur," she said a few seconds later. "I'm Liesel."

"And I am Helga Shorenstein. It's very nice to meet both of you. You're not Jewish, are you?"

"No, but my fiancé is."

"I would like very much to meet him," Helga said.

"That won't be possible. Flem went back to Copenhagen to smuggle more Jews across the Sound."

"Oh, I see," Helga said. "Well, good for him. I will pray for his success and his safety."

"Thank you." Liesel turned to her father. "I was about to take Greta outside for some fresh air and quiet. Would you like to join us?"

"I would indeed," he said.

Outside, it was sunny but crisp. Liesel gazed wistfully into the sky wondering what Flem was doing. Did he miss her as much as she missed him?

"Cheer up, *yndling*," her father said. "Everything will be better soon, and a lot more comfortable once we've moved into the hotel."

"It's not that, Father. I was just missing Flem. Besides, I doubt we'll be able to afford to move into a hotel."

"Rosa Bertman has convinced the owner to make half of his rooms available to Danish refugees at no charge."

"Are you serious?"

"Ask her yourself," he said, leading his daughter to a bench in the middle of the garden.

"That woman is a saint," Liesel said as she sat down.

"A saint indeed. Thanks to Rosa others have been opening their homes as well. She's even organized a fundraiser that will provide ration cards to refugees."

Liesel eyes filled with tears as she gazed down at the sleeping infant. "They'll certainly be a blessing with so many fleeing Denmark."

Her father sighed. "Yes, and with little more than the clothes on their backs."

"Do you think Flem will try to find us the next time he drops off refugees?"

"That all depends on how much time he has."

"I've been thinking I might go down to the dock where he dropped us off and wait for him there."

"You can't do that, *yndling*!"

"Sweden is setting up refugee camps there. They're asking for volunteers to process new arrivals. I have to do something, Father."

"Go back to school."

"But I want to see Flem."

Her father sighed, and they fell silent for several minutes.

"What will you do once your wound is healed?" Liesel asked.

"The Swedish government plans to send refugees on to Malmo after they're processed here in Helsingborg. They'll need a doctor."

"A refugee camp won't pay much."

"Your mother wants to help, too."

"Mother? Working?" Liesel could hardly believe her ears.

"Your mother is a capable woman, my dear."

"I know, but she's never worked."

"And just what do you call raising you and your brother?"

"You know what I mean, Father."

"Of course, I do," he said wincing as he slipped his arm around her shoulder.

"You're still having a lot of pain, aren't you?"

"Only when I move," he said, forcing a smile.

"You should have it checked."

"I'm a doctor, Liesel."

"You're also a patient," she pointed out.

"I want you to go with us to Malmo. You can volunteer there at the camp."

"But Flem would never find me in Malmo."

"You could send him word through the Underground."

"I mean when he drops off refugees."

"Well, I don't want us splitting up."

"I'm not a child, Father. I'm almost a married woman," she reminded him as the infant in her arms began to stir. "Besides, the Lunds will be here."

"I don't like it, Liesel. I'm losing my family, first Aldur, now you."

Liesel felt her father's torture but remained adamant all the same. "The war won't last forever, Father. We'll be together again. I know it."

"I almost lost your mother."

"But you didn't!"

"She never would've been arrested if it hadn't been for me. You saw what they did to her."

"You did what you had to do, Father. Mother is proud of you, and so am I, even Aldur."

Tears filled her father's eyes. "I'm scared, *yndling*. I've seen first-hand how quickly our lives can change."

~*~*~

Sunday, 03 October, 1943

Holding tightly to the letter in his hand, Pastor Uri stood behind the pulpit. His church was packed that first Sunday in October. Knowing what he was about to read, he wasn't sure if the tension he felt came from him or his flock.

He cleared his throat. "By now, I am sure everyone has heard what has happened to our countrymen and that this atrocity distresses you as much as it does me."

A wave of agreement rippled through the congregation. Pastor Uri waited for it to die down before he continued.

"In response to this atrocity, our bishops have written a letter to Dr. Werner Best, expressing our dissent. Today, in every Lutheran Church throughout Denmark, our pastors will be reading this condemnation," he said, waving the sheet of paper in his hand. He cleared his throat and began to read:

"We must never forget that the Lord Jesus Christ was born in Bethlehem of the Virgin Mary, according to God's promise to His Chosen People. Their persecution conflicts with the Church's teaching. We are to love our neighbors as ourselves. Christ taught us that all men have value. This persecution of the Jews conflicts not only with our doctrine but with our history.

"Under Danish law, all citizens are granted religious freedom. We Danes respect the right of people to worship in accordance with their conscience. Neither race nor religion should deprive a citizen of these rights, nor of their liberty or property. Notwithstanding our separate religious beliefs, we Lutherans will fight to preserve these precious freedoms for all of our Jewish neighbors. We value these rights as much as we value life."

With that, the congregation stood to its feet applauding. Many were in tears as they showed their solidarity with what was just read. Choking up at his flock's overwhelming response, Pastor Uri waited until everyone sat down before he continued.

"The Danish Church comprehends its duty to be law-abiding citizens, but when man's laws are corrupt, we are bound by our conscience to obey God rather than men."

Pastor Uri laid his letter on the podium. He pulled out his handkerchief, removed his glasses and dried his eyes. Then he waited for everyone to calm down.

"Many claim that politics must never be mixed with religion, and under this occupation, I certainly understand why."

Several in the congregation shouted, "Amen!"

"That said, I can assure you that what you have just heard read to you this Sunday morning has been read in every Lutheran Church throughout Denmark. This had to be declared," he said, waving the page again, "regardless of the cost. Many of us might be arrested, many of us may lose our lives. But I'd rather die defending Danish citizens than live in silence knowing I allowed evil to triumph."

At that, the congregation stood to their feet and cheered.

~*~*~

Near midnight, deep in the woods off the coast of Elsinore, Flem lay on the ground with forty of his compatriots. Families snuggled next to their loved ones, under wool blankets, trying to keep warm for a couple of hours before their scheduled crossing.

Unable to turn off his thoughts, Flem stared up at the stars. So much had happened so quickly, and except for his engagement to Liesel, most of it had been terrible, yet Flem had never felt more alive. He understood, for the first time, what Scripture meant by praying without ceasing. Leaning not on one's own understanding but in all things acknowledging God would never again be just a Psalm. His life and the lives of others depended on his maintaining communication with the Lord.

In crossing after crossing, with as many as twenty refugees hidden aboard, never once had Katlev's cutter been stopped. It was as if the Most High had rendered them invisible and not just them but many others. Even the Underground, though not particularly religious, had declared Denmark's rescue of the Jews a miracle.

Next to Flem, Katlev mumbled in his sleep, then sat up suddenly.

"Are you okay?" Flem whispered, not wanting to disturb the others all around him.

"I had another dream," Katlev said.

"About Jacob?"

"He kept calling my name, begging me to save him."

"You have to stop tormenting yourself," Flem said, sitting up.

"God controls dreams," the old man replied.

"Could you keep it down?" a man off to his left said. "We're trying to sleep."

"Sorry," Flem said, then whispered to Katlev, "Come on. Let's go for a walk so we can talk."

With only the moon to light their way, Flem and Katlev maneuvered around sleeping bodies, then proceeded deeper into the woods.

"We need to pray about these nightmares you keep having, Katlev."

"They're from God."

"Maybe, maybe not," Flem said then noticed a beam of light zigzagging in the underbrush. "Who goes there?" he asked, knowing that at this distance, if it was an enemy, God alone could save them.

"I bring you a warning from Aldur."

Flem breathed easy again, recognizing Ove's voice. "Is Aldur okay?"

"He's fine," Ove said, coming out of the brush. "But you need to get everyone ready to leave now. Load as many as you can, then come back for the rest before dawn. The Germans will start sweeping this area right after sunrise."

"We'll never get all of them across in that time," Flem said.

"The Underground is sending you another boat. It should be here any minute. We have three beach houses, about 20 kilometers east of here, that you can use to hide the rest. Here are the keys." Ove handed them to Flem. "I also have this." He reached into his jacket and pulled out an envelope. "It's for you," he said, passing it to Katlev. "Your mailman thought it might be important. He's one of us."

"It's from Palestine," Katlev said.

"It must be from your friend, Matityahu. Well, what are you waiting for?" Flem asked. "Open it!"

"Here! You can use my torch." Ove handed it to Katlev.

When Katlev finished reading, he folded his letter and slipped it into his pocket.

"Well, what did he say?" Flem asked.

"He heard from a man whose brother was hiding Jacob in Germany."

"See!" Flem said. "I told you not to worry."

"Jacob was sent to a concentration camp in Czechoslovakia two weeks ago."

"That's where they were planning to send us," Flem said. "But Ha Shem had a different plan."

"Did He?" Katlev asked, sending chills down Flem's back. "I'm not so sure…"

Chapter Thirty-one

"It's a miracle!" Nettie exclaimed as they sat in the tiny kitchenette in their suite. Sol lowered his newspaper and stared at her over his spectacles.

"Isn't it wonderful? They just keep coming and coming. It is a miracle."

"A miracle," Sol said, "requires a God. I no longer believe in such a being." He lowered his gaze and returned to his reading.

"That's blasphemy, Sol! You don't mean it!"

"Blasphemy? And just what do you call your idolatry of this Jesus?"

"He's our promised Messiah, Sol, the very one you've prayed all your life would come. Well, He did, and He will come again."

"You don't know what you're talking about, woman!"

"I know what Maimonides said in his second article of faith. He said, that the Creator—blessed be He!—is *Echad*, and that there is no Unity like His."

"What's your point?" Sol demanded, indignant that his wife would dare quote Maimonides in defense of her idolatry.

"*Echad* means a compound unity, Sol! It's why Bereshith 1:26 says, "Let Us make man in Our image, according to Our likeness.""

Sol had heard enough. He pounded the table. "That crazy fisherman is behind this. He's the one filling your head with these heresies."

188

"You just told me you no longer believe there is a God. Well, if God doesn't exist, Sol, why do you care who I pray to?"
"I don't! Not anymore! Why should I? But I still recognize truth. And the truth is this, I have no son, no wife, no home, no job, and no country!"

~*~*~

That afternoon, in one of the beach houses, Flem stretched out all six feet of his aching body in the first real bed he had lain in in a week. He needed to sleep but could not stop ruminating about the eighty Jews who'd been arrested that morning, while hiding in the attic of a church in Gilleleje. Some turncoat had turned them in for a reward offered by Werner Best.

Flem knew he must let the defeats go and focus on the miracles, like the hospital in Copenhagen that had become a clearinghouse for Jews. Ambulance drivers would collect them and have them checked in under an alias. They would be held there until arrangements could be made to transport them to various remote locations where they would rendezvous with the Underground. Then they would be driven to the docks and hidden on fishing boats, the only civilian watercraft not ordered into dry-dock by the German High Command.

A bookstore in downtown Copenhagen, right across the street from Gestapo Headquarters, was another triumph. Its secret room in the back hid Jews right under the Reich's nose. Miracles were endless. Nearly everyone in Denmark was doing something, most of it was impromptu. Sabotage had escalated as well, in spite of the Reich's crackdown. The Nazis had pushed Danes too far. Now Danes, no longer Hitler's pampered canary, were pushing back.

Giving up on trying to fall asleep, Flem got out of bed. He would write a letter to Liesel and find someone to deliver it to her the next time he docked in Sweden.

~*~*~

Theresienstadt Concentration Camp

Jacob lay on his hard cot trying to sleep. He covered his face, hoping the blanket would filter out the stench of burning flesh, but it didn't. Dreams were his only escape. They took him back to happier days from his past, wonderful days he had spent with Sima. If only he could stay with her forever. Only, last night his dream of lovely Sima was different. She had spoken to him about Yeshua.

~*~*~

"We have to move everyone out of here tonight," Ove told Flem when he returned from town.

"Okay. We'll sail as soon as it's dark."

"Not from here you won't." Ove removed his cap. "Every village along the coast is crawling with Gestapo, including Snekkersten and Humlebæk."

Flem's stomach knotted. "Are you telling me we're trapped?"

"We're going to die here, aren't we?" an older woman cried. Her husband draped his arm about her shoulder as others began reacting to the news.

"We've made it this far. We can't lose heart now," another woman said.

"We're going to have to relocate you to a couple of smaller fishing villages further south," Ove said. "It'll be safer there...for now at least."

"Klintholm and Moen?" Katlev asked.

"That is correct," Ove replied.

"You know these places?" Flem asked.

"It's been a while," Katlev said, "but I do."

"The distance across the Sound is greater than it is here," Ove said, taking off his overcoat, "but it's our safest bet for now."

"How will we get there without being spotted by the Gestapo?" someone asked.

"Just before sunset, I'll drive the milk truck back to town and call my contact," Ove told them. "He'll send out an ambulance. You should all be able to fit in."

"What about my boat? Can I sail it to Klintholm with the Gestapo out in full force?" Katlev asked.

Ove shifted his weight, looking troubled. "You need to see this." He pulled back the blackout drape. In the distance, beyond the cove, where Katlev had docked his boat, smoke billowed into the sky.

Watching Katlev's face drain of color, Flem's heart broke.

"Don't worry, Katlev," Ove said. "We have other boats we can use."

Just then a baby that had been fussing earlier began to squall.

"Make it stop, or we'll all be arrested!" someone yelled.

"No, we won't," Ove said. "Once you are in the ambulance a doctor will give all children under four a sedative. It'll quiet them for several hours."

"Is it safe?" Flem asked.

"Safer than having the Gestapo hear the crying," Ove replied.

Satisfied, Flem went over to comfort the old man. "You'll get another boat, Katlev, bigger and faster, only not so loud."

"No, I won't."

"Of course, you will. Sweden sells boats, even to Jewish fishermen."

"I don't need a boat anymore. The Most High has another plan."

Remembering the letter from Palestine, Flem's mouth went dry. "You can't do this, Katlev! It's suicide!"

"I can't run this time, Flem."

"Are you absolutely certain this is Yah's plan?" Flem asked as tears filled his eyes.

"Any doubts I might've had burned up with my boat."

"The Nazis burned your boat, Katlev! Not God!"

"No, Flem. You're wrong. I'm turning myself in."

"They'll send you to a camp!"

Katlev laid his hand on Flem's arm. "Not just any camp. Jacob will be there."

191

"What about saving Jews here?"

"You and others will continue that work."

"But I don't want you to go!"

"If I don't, what will happen to Jacob?" Katlev asked.

No longer fighting back his tears, Flem grabbed his friend in a bear hug. "How soon are you turning yourself in?" he asked when he finally let him go.

"Tomorrow morning. Tonight, I'm writing my will. I'll be leaving the house to you and Liesel. Of course, as long as the Nazis are in charge, it won't be safe for you to live there."

"It doesn't matter. We'll be in Sweden."

"You'll be back, son. This is your home."

Chapter Thirty-two

By October 31, 1943, weighing fifteen pounds less than when he first went into hiding, Flem docked in Sweden with his final boatload of refugees. Three days later, on the 3rd of November, he made Liesel his wife in a church in Malmo. Both families had been in attendance, even Aldur who was not able to stay long for fear of being missed.

Flem and Liesel exchanged vows under a *chuppah*. According to the pastor, it was the first Jewish wedding ever held in his church. The couple had insisted on sticking to their original plan, the one cooked up that day on the old man's cutter. It was their way of honoring Katlev's presence.

Tragically for Flem, the reverse was true for his father. Sol Lund was there but only in body. On a happier note, they learned on their wedding day that only 472 Jews out of Denmark's 7,500 were in Theresienstadt Concentration Camp. The rest were safely in Sweden.

~*~*~

Two Years Later
Friday, 13 April, 1945

When an automobile flying the Swedish flag arrived at Theresienstadt Concentration Camp, rumors started flying. At first Jacob did not believe them, even though the day before, the Germans had ordered the camp cleaned. That usually meant putting on a charade for the Red Cross inspection team. On such occasions, prisoners were treated humanely and fed generous portions of decent food. Of course, that only lasted a few hours. But if Jacob had learned anything these past two long years, it was how to be grateful for little things.

Edelstein rushed into the barracks, with more color in his cheeks than Jacob had ever seen.

"Have you heard? All Danish prisoners are to assemble on the camp square tonight."

"What for? Another one of their free-for-alls?" Jacob asked, still grieving about the last.

"It's all been arranged between Bernadotte and Himmler. The Danes will be released in two days!"

"Heinrich Himmler? Are you certain?" Jacob had barely gotten the question out when a German officer entered their barracks.

"Jacob Mitzger, you are to come with me."

Praying silently, he followed the soldier to the Commandant's office, where he was instructed to wait with a bench full of other prisoners, who looked as confused as Jacob felt. Something was definitely up, and since that usually was not good, he prayed even more fervently.

After twenty minutes, the Commandant called his name. Jacob approached his desk.

"Here." The Commandant handed him a form. "Sign this!"

"What is it?"

"Your statement that your stay here has been a productive and happy one."

"But I don't understand."

The Commandant pounded the desk. "You stupid Jew, sign!"

Jacob picked up the fountain pen and did as he was ordered.

"You will leave with the Danes the day after tomorrow."

"But I am German."

"With friends in Copenhagen. One of them has been pulling strings. Now get out of here! Go!"

Miracle Across the Sound

~*~*~

Before boarding their buses, the Danes gave away what remained of the food items and medicine they had been receiving in packages from Denmark on a regular basis since their arrival in the camp. Word was that King Christian had demanded his countrymen be allowed to send them. Then inexplicably, right after his old friend Katlev Hertz showed up, Jacob began receiving them too, addressed to Uncle Jacob. And now he—with the Danes—was on the way to Malmo in Sweden. Only first, they had to pass through northern Germany and Denmark.

Jacob peered out the window, horrified by the utter devastation that he saw. Once-great cities now lay in ruin. The Reich's thousand-year reign had been reduced to rubble in just five years. Now Hitler's recruits consisted of old men and young boys who toted rifles on bombed-out streets. What madness, Jacob thought. What depravity!

Sickened by what he saw outside his window, Jacob was about to pull down his shade when several S.S. officers saved him the effort. Hurriedly, they moved through the bus, snapping down the shades in their final act of censorship. But no one on the bus complained. Why should they? They all knew they were on their way to freedom. Jacob wanted to rejoice with them, but his heart still grieved the loss of his friend.

Once the caravan of Swedish buses with red crosses painted on their sides had passed through the German border every shade went back up. And this time they stayed up, through the frontier and into Denmark. There, thousands of people lined the roads waving Danish flags.

When their bus slowed to a stop, everyone on board opened their window as Danes on the street shouted, "Welcome to Denmark!"

Jacob had never seen anything like it. Soon the crowd was passing them gifts. Flowers, cigarettes, and chocolates passed through the bus's open windows. A young woman in a yellow dress passed Jacob a bottle of milk, something he'd not tasted in a long

195

time. With tears in his eyes, Jacob removed the paper cap and pressed the bottle to his mouth. The cool, wonderful liquid went down smoothly, but then, as everyone on the bus began singing the Danish national anthem, Jacob began to cough.

Finally, the buses started moving again. In every hamlet, similar scenes occurred, until they reached Copenhagen, where crowds of thousands became hundreds of thousands. Slowly the buses made their way onward to the docks. There they would board boats bound for Sweden.

Jacob felt sorry for the Danes. How they must long to stay put in their homeland. Only they couldn't. The war wasn't over, not officially, even though everyone knew Germany had lost. The Reich's thousand-year reign had finally ended, Jacob thought as he started coughing again. Was it from all the excitement, or from all those freezing nights in the camp? He wasn't sure. All he knew was that he couldn't stop and that everyone around him was staring. That was when he noticed that the red stain on his handkerchief was blood.

~*~*~

Copenhagen
Six Months Later

Soon Shabbat would begin, Flem thought as he tucked his six-month old son into bed. It hardly seemed possible that two years had passed since Katlev's boat was torched by the Nazis. He and Liesel moved into the house when they returned from Sweden after the war ended in Europe. But with all of the changes made, the freshly painted walls, the new drapes and rugs, memories of the old man still filled every room, especially tonight.

Flem could not stop thinking about him, or the grief that had gripped him back in April as he and Liesel waited for Katlev on the dock. His absence left a gaping hole in Flem's heart and so many questions unanswered. Did Jacob accept Yeshua? Not everyone who hears the Good News does. His own father was proof of that, Flem thought with a sigh. He glanced at his watch. It was almost the Sabbath. He had to stop ruminating.

Both families were already gathered. The table was set, and the aroma of freshly baked challah bread filled the house. Soon Liesel would don her scarf and light the candles to welcome in Shabbat. It was a time to rejoice, not to mourn the past, Flem chided himself as someone knocked on their door.

"Shall I answer that?" Flem's mother called from the parlor.

"Please do," Liesel said.

Flem followed his wife into the dining room. The table was set with a white linen cloth given to them as a wedding present. The china was a gift from her parents. As usual, Liesel had outdone herself. Even her challah bread looked like it had been braided by a professional. She had just placed the embroidered, white satin challah cover over the two loaves of bread when his mother-in-law led an elderly gentleman into their dining room.

"Forgive me for arriving unannounced, but I just got released from the convalescent home, and Katlev made me promise to spend my first Shabbat in freedom with you."

"You must be Jacob Mitzger!" Flem said, offering his hand then quickly decided a hug was more fitting. He opened his arms, and Jacob returned the embrace like a long-lost member of the family.

"I'm Fleming Lund, by the way."

"I was certain of it," Jacob said with a smile. "Now, let me see if I can name the rest of you. Katlev described all of you so well."

Flem wanted to ask him about Katlev but decided to let Jacob have his fun. When he finished naming everyone correctly except Aldur's fiancée, Marlene, Liesel kindled the Sabbath candles and welcomed in the Sabbath with prayer.

"Blessed are you, Adonai Eloheinu, King of the Universe, who sanctifies us with your commandments and commands us to light the candles of Shabbat."

When she finished, Flem lifted the Kiddush cup. "And there was evening and morning, a sixth day. The heavens and earth were finished, the whole host of them, and on the seventh day God rested.

He blessed and sanctified the seventh day because in it he had rested from his work. Blessed are You, Adonai Eloheinu, King of the Universe, who creates the fruit of the vine."

Everyone said, "Amen," and sipped wine from the Kiddush cup.

Then, Flem raised the two loaves and repeated the ancient blessing. "Blessed are you, Adonai Eloheinu, King of the Universe, who brings forth bread from the earth."

Everyone said, "Amen."

When it came time to eat, Jacob sat next to Flem's father.

Flem raised his glass to Jacob. "Rabbi, I hope you will enjoy my wife's cooking. Your presence makes this night even more special."

Flem's father laid down his fork. "Are you really a rabbi?" he asked, shocking everyone at the table, for he rarely said a word, much less asked a question.

"I am. But please, call me Jacob. I have no family left, you see, except those of you here. My dearest friend bequeathed you to me."

That was when Flem knew for certain that Katlev was dead.

"And family members," Jacob continued, "call each other by their first names. Do they not?"

His father's countenance again became an expressionless mask. He picked up his knife and fork and began cutting off a piece of meat. It was an awkward moment, especially for Jacob. Flem was relieved when Marlene changed the subject.

"Were you surprised to get packages addressed to Uncle Jacob?"

"I was indeed. Delighted too," Jacob told her.

"That was the rule, I'm afraid," Marlene went on to explain. "You see, when the Germans finally agreed to the King's demands that Danes be allowed to send food and medicine, it was stipulated that they be sent only to family members."

Jacob smiled. "So that's how I became an uncle."

Later when conversation turned to life in the camp, Flem asked Jacob if he was surprised to see Katlev.

Jacob laid down his fork. "No, I was expecting him." He turned to Flem's father. "Did you know that I had lost my faith?"

After a moment, Sol stopped staring at his plate to look at Jacob.

"It was hard after the night of broken glass for me to believe in a loving God. Life in Germany had become horrific."

Sol remained silent.

"The truth is I had become bitter many years before. In the camp, I grew worse. Then I started having dreams—at first about a young woman who died long ago, then about Katlev. Finding my dearest friend was no surprise, but learning how he got there was."

"He was a Jew," Sol said, "at least as far as the Germans were concerned."

"You don't know then?" Jacob asked.

"Know what?" Sol said.

"Katlev gave himself up when he learned I was there."

"Nonsense!" Sol said.

"It's true, Father. I tried my best to talk him out of it the day the Nazis burned his boat, but Katlev was adamant. He was convinced that the Most High had a mission for him."

"You see, Katlev was having dreams about me, long before he knew I was there. He turned himself in to beg my forgiveness and to do what the Most High called him to do many years ago."

"What was that?" Sol asked.

Jacob then told him about Sima and about what happened after Katlev failed to keep his appointment that tragic afternoon.

"He fled here," Flem said, "hoping to be swallowed by a fish, like Jonah."

"He knew, of course," Jacob said, "that Yeshua had forgiven him, but it broke his heart all the same."

"For the rest of his life, Katlev tried to make up for it," Liesel added. "He loved everyone."

Flem's mother and Mrs. Prestur agreed, even Aldur.

After that everyone grew silent for a time. Then his father asked, "Is it true? Did Katlev really study to be a rabbi?"

"It's true, and he would have made a great one."

"How did he die?" Sol asked.

"The S.S. organized one of their monthly free-for-alls, forcing the frailest among us to draw lots. When Katlev saw what I had drawn, he bribed the officer in charge so that he could take my place."

"Bribed him with what?" Sol asked.

"One of his care packages. The S.S. forced us to attend and watch them beat each other up."

"How could they do that?" Flem said, unable to imagine such depravity.

"The S.S. ordered it. If anyone refused, the Nazis would pummel them. So, everyone complied, everyone that is except Katlev." Here Jacob's voice began to tremble. "Katlev looked like raw meat by the end of the melee, and the next morning he never woke up. My dearest friend gave his life to save mine."

"Just like Yeshua," Flem said as tears filled his eyes. When his father broke down and began sobbing, Flem finally understood his mentor's calling. HaShem, in His unsearchable ways, had seen fit to use the sacrificial love of a determined old fisherman to soften his father's heart. "Well done, Katlev," Flem whispered. "Well done!"

THE END

Author Bio

 Christine Egbert is a retired RN who fell in love with reading through Nancy Drew novels. At fourteen, she decided one day she would become a writer of the kind of inspiring stories she loved to get lost in. Only, her life choices postponed that desire until she was in her fifties. That's when she first began honing her craft.

As a Christian, she wanted to write wholesome fiction. And for four years, when she wasn't writing, she devoured books about writing. Today, she has one bookcase filled entirely with nothing but how-to-write-fiction books on everything imaginable—voice, style, character development, interior monologue, point of view, dialogue, creating conflict and suspense, pacing, and plotting.

As par for the course, she claims her first three novels were terrible. Rereading them made her teeth hurt. She thinks her third wasn't bad. But it was her fourth novel, *Miracle Across The Sound*, a historical WWII novel about Denmark saving most of its Jewish citizens, three years into its occupation, that she knew would one day be published, and now that day has arrived.

Betrothed

Messianic Imprint of Little Roni Publishers
Clanton, Alabama
www.littleronipublishers.com

Little Roni Publishers' *Betrothed* Imprint has been created and set apart to the glory of Yeshua Ha Mashiach, our God and King.

Isaiah 58:12 | Galatians 2:20

More Titles from Betrothed

Apologetics / Hebraic Roots
Contending for the Faith, Christine Egbert

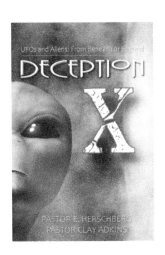

Eschatology / End Times / Alien Deception
Deception X & *Revelation 9,11*, by Rabbi Eric Herschberg

Made in the USA
Las Vegas, NV
02 May 2024